For The Love of Faith

By Tricia McGill

Print ISBNs
Amazon Print 978-0-2286-2308-3
LSI Print 978-0-2286-2309-0
B&N Print 978-0-2286-2310-6

BWL Publishing Inc.

Books we love to write ...
Authors around the world.

http://bwlpublishing.ca

Dedication

To brave adventurers everywhere

Chapter One

Ballarat, Victoria. 1860

Faith quickened her pace as she neared the store, her Ma's list clutched in her hand. This visit had become the highlight of her week, for the anticipation reached a level she could not understand. She sincerely hoped that the owner's son, one Walter Finch would be working behind the counter. The store contained everything from cooking ingredients for the women, to shovels and hats for the men working out at the diggings, and had taken on a new pleasure in the past few months. She was at a loss to understand quite why this should be.

Previously Walt had barely passed the time of day with her until one morning as she handed her list over to George Finch, his son had come out of the back room, wiping his hands on a scrap of rag. "Finished out there, boy?" his father asked and with a nod Walt came towards Faith and smiled—and her heart was lost as he asked after her welfare and made some comment on her appearance that completely took her aback. Until that morning, no lad of similar age had shown the slightest interest in her and certainly not in her state of health.

Suddenly the one who now seemed to fill her thoughts far too often was striding towards her. Too late to step from the firmer path that had been laid down in front of the shops to protect the boots of the ladies, and to head across the street. Probably best, as after the heavy October rain overnight her only boots would soon be mud spattered, giving her Ma something new to complain about. Spare money for clothing was scarce these days according to her Ma, so these boots would need to last a few more winters.

Nothing for it now but to come face to face with him. She pulled the brim of her bonnet low over her face in an effort to cover the blush she knew was rising. Would she ever get used to the horrors attached to having a skin that her mother often likened to oatmeal? Her Ma put it down to her English background, and one of her main aims in life was to ensure that Faith kept her complexion from becoming shrivelled by the often-blazing sunshine before she reached full maturity. Her Ma had a thousand rules she lived by, far too many for Faith to keep up with at times.

Already Walter Finch was heading unerringly it seemed straight to her, so there was no escape. "Good day to you Mistress Boswell," he said with a distinct chuckle in his voice to prove that once again he was likely set on teasing her.

"Good morning, Mister Finch," she mumbled, side stepping to dodge his nearness. Of course, as always, he was out to confuse her by standing far too close for what good manners dictated. Often Faith considered these rules of etiquette so out of place in this land that abounded with scoundrels, hard-working miners, and bushrangers. Not that she ever had been confronted by a bushranger—but according to her Ma's reasoning, just because she had never come across one did not mean they were not out there waiting to rob, or worse, ravish every female they met.

"You are looking particularly fetching on this dull old day, I must say, and a sight for these sore eyes." Doffing his wide-brimmed hat Walt added a small bow, as if he was some gentleman of high breeding. According to Faith's Ma, Walt, his father George, plus his mother Daisy, were living a pretense. Just because they owned one of the most important establishments in town—a shop that included just about everything needed by most inhabitants of the area, did not give them the right to think they were aristocracy or at least above their station in life according to her Ma.

Rather, Gertrude insisted they were no better than she was, just lower-class folk trying to earn an honest living. Faith often wondered just why, if that was her Ma's opinion, she put on false airs and graces herself. Not that Faith would have the temerity to ask her Ma such. Faith knew Walt's sister Florrie well, for she was of similar age and a likeable girl. Faith had also met their Mama, Daisy, and thought her kind and loving towards her family and always polite to their customers. Faith could not understand her own Ma's reasoning. Although she insisted they were lower class, her set of rules at times commanded Faith behave as if she was a countess or of some higher rank.

"A small birdie told me that someone is nearing a special birthday. Seventeen is an age for rejoicing." With a devilish grin, Walt bowed again, sending a lock of his thick dark hair across his forehead. As he straightened, he flicked this back carelessly.

"How so? It is just another number— nothing at all to rejoice about," she remarked pertly, although inside she did feel that this birthday was rather special indeed. A few of the girls of similar age around the town and diggings were already wed or planning to wed their beaus by the time they reached her age. Mind you, by her Ma's reasoning a lot of them wed for reasons of convenience rather than affection.

"By that I presume that your mother has no plans for a big celebration for her only daughter." Faith could not be certain, but thought she heard a touch of disdain in that statement. "Florrie has been enjoying parties most of her life and our Ma would not dream of letting such an important occasion go by without at least inviting a clutch of her friends to celebrate along with her. It was she who told me that she was waiting on an invitation to your festivities."

Faith chewed on her fingertip, unsure how to answer him. In fact, he knew that Faith had been one of the friends invited to Florrie's sixteenth birthday celebration last year. It was on that afternoon when Walt had first seemed to realise Faith was not a silly child anymore. At the time, Faith had become confused and flummoxed by his attentions while inside she felt as if a hundred butterflies fluttered there. Because she had never attended school, as her Ma had been her only teacher, there had not been a lot of chance to mix with many of her own age, boy or girl. It had pleased her no end when Florrie befriended her after meeting her at the store one day. She did learn that day that Walt was about three years her senior, and to Faith he seemed to possess more self-assurance than she ever would.

"Ma is too busy with the many chores the lodging house demands of her to worry about celebrating the passing of a year of her daughter's life." Even as she said the words, Faith knew that nonetheless inside it did hurt.

"How is it that your Ma has no husband to assist her?" He put a hand on Faith's arm as he rushed to add, "I apologise if that is too impertinent a question. But most women who arrive here in the diggings follow their menfolk, few come alone."

"I thought it was common knowledge that my Pa died after coming here and setting up the lodging house—about three years ago." It shamed Faith but truth was, her Pa died in a fight with a miner over a gambling debt. She never found out the whole truth as her Ma refused to talk about it—likely because she too was ashamed to admit she had married a gambling man who drank to excess.

Pa had never favoured Faith with a lot of attention, and although she knew her parents did argue a lot behind the door of their bedroom, he had never been unkind to her. As far as she knew he was not a brute of a man, but she felt that somehow her Ma did not grieve excessively over his passing. As luck would have it, she knew how to run the business, so managed adequately without him around.

"Oh. I am sorry; I am not one to listen to idle gossip."

Although his statement sounded genuine, deep-down Faith had a suspicion that he already knew what fate befell her Pa. "I have to get on," she said as she waved a hand.

"I do hope I haven't upset you." He did seem perturbed, but as Faith knew little about boys, there was a chance he was perhaps chiding her.

"My Mama will be wondering where I am if I linger too long."

"Perhaps we will bump into each other later. I just have a small errand to run for my Pa and will then head back to the store. I presume that is where you are headed." He nodded at the list still clutched in her hand.

"Perhaps." Feigning nonchalance, she waved the hand holding the scrap of paper and with head bent scurried off. She had not gone far when she heard Walt greeting another young woman—one Grace Barker, daughter of the tobacconist. A feeling of something akin to jealousy swept through Faith, which was ridiculous as he obviously showed the same attention to everyone who shopped in his parent's store. It was likely the way he had been taught. Something her Mama had taught Faith was that it was only common sense that they showed civility to everyone who was, or was likely to be, a paying customer.

That feeling of jealousy stayed with Faith as she entered the Finch's family store. Two women waiting to be served greeted her civilly before continuing their conversations. The miners and those seeking large fortunes, who came and went as regularly as the seasons, were the ones Mama warned her not to socialise with. Not that Faith would readily have a chance to mingle with such folk, for her Ma ensured that she kept well away from the diggings or drinking establishments that these types seemed to throng to when not slogging away at their digs.

To her disappointment, Walt did not return while she was being served by Daisy Finch. "We'll have the order delivered first thing," Mrs. Finch said as Faith turned to go, after spending a few moments more chatting to Florrie who was in the process of arranging tins on a shelf.

"Thank you, and good day to you." Mother and daughter waved her on her way and even though Faith knew she would likely get a lashing from her Ma's tongue for being away for so long, she dawdled home in the hope that she would bump into Walt again. There was still a chance that he would likely make their delivery in the morning, and that thought sustained her.

"You took your time, my girl," her Ma scolded the moment Faith entered and removed her bonnet. "There are a million chores awaiting and you have been dallying—no doubt chatting foolishly to that Florrie, a brainless chit if ever there was one."

"But you taught me to be polite to folk, Mama, and I could not rush away when she so obviously wanted to talk. And she is not brainless at all, but very polite and easy to talk to."

"Piffle." Muttering to herself, her Ma went on into the kitchen where their cook, Bertha, was preparing dinner for the residents. Miners and their families who had been at the diggings for any length of time were mostly now settled in their makeshift homes made of bark, but some newcomers still lived in tents, the thought of which made Faith shudder. How they survived the cold nights in winter she could not imagine. The ones who stayed in their lodging house were mostly travellers passing through town or newcomers who hadn't yet staked their claim. A widow woman in her middle years who had been here a few months, had lost her husband before he had time to stake his claim, and currently she was their only long-term boarder.

"Don't let your Ma upset you, dearie," Bertha advised as she stirred a pot on the stove. "She worries about you, too many rough sorts passing through town." With a heavy sigh, she put the stirring spoon down and patted Faith on the arm. "How about a warm drink, it's a bit chilly out there today." Without waiting for an answer, she placed the kettle on the stove top. It might have been chilly out on the street but so much heat came from the fire blazing in the old stove that it was as warm as a mid-summer day here in the kitchen.

Faith nodded. "I'll just pop along to my room and take off my jacket." She went out and along the passage to the room she shared with her Ma at the back of the house. Just about the smallest room in the house, it was cramped and stuffy with a tiny window high up on the outer wall, so therefore unsuitable for the paying customers. Apart from the two narrow beds, they shared a dresser and a table just large enough to hold a small mirror. The cupboard was barely large enough for their sparse clothing, so depending on the season, some of their few outfits were tucked away in a chest in the tiny space beneath the stairs.

With a sigh, Faith stared at her face in the scratched mirror, as she longed once again for a room to call her own. Before Pa passed, she had slept in this room alone and relished it, but now the room her parents had shared was kept for the guests.

Later as Faith, Ma and Bertha sat at the kitchen table eating their meal, once the residents had all been served, Faith asked tentatively, "Mama, would it be possible to invite a few of my friends for afternoon tea to celebrate my birthday with me?"

"Whatever for?" Her Mama's tone did not bode well for a satisfactory outcome.

"Well, I was invited to Florrie Finch's birthday party and thought it would be nice to return the invitation, seeing as I am turning seventeen."

"What has that got to do with anything?" she snapped. Faith stared down at her plate, wondering once again why it was that her Ma had become so bitter. Of course, becoming a widow when you were just on thirty years of age must have been difficult, but some of the women who shared the diggings with their menfolk were on their second husbands, so she heard, when their first was killed when a shaft collapsed on them, or similar tragedies. Also, it wasn't as if her Ma was heartbroken at her loss. There were times when Faith suspected that her own birth was not particularly a cause for joy either.

"Oh, that would be lovely, dearie; I could bake a nice special cake and add a few delicacies, Missus." Bertha grinned at the prospect as she looked across at her employer. "And what about inviting that nice young man, Florrie's brother, what's his name?"

"Walter?" Faith felt her cheeks hot up as she blurted out his name without thinking. Her Ma's face seemed to stiffen even more than usual as she stared at them both as if they had suggested inviting the Governor and his wife.

As if suddenly reaching a decision, her Mama said, "Well I suppose you could invite the three of them, but no more, mind, we don't want the house full of young people and their accompanying noise to disturb the residents."

Bertha seemed just as surprised as Faith by this change of mind and said as she rubbed her hands together, "Lovely, tell me what cakes you would like, Faith dear, and what day you want to invite your friends and I will plan a nice feast."

Gertrude muttered something but no more was said as they finished their meal. As they cleared the table in the guests' dining room, a knock came on the front door. In the process of carrying dishes out to the kitchen, Gert said over a shoulder, "Answer that Faith. Lord knows who would be calling at this time of night."

Faith nodded as she went out and along the passage. It was barely nine o clock and often people turned up at all odd hours depending on when they arrived in town, so as usual her Ma's retort seemed to have no reasoning behind it. "Yes, can I be of assistance," she asked of the tall stranger who stood on the step, his face barely discernible in the fading light.

His voice was pleasant, denoting a person of good breeding as he said, "I am seeking one Gertrude Boswell, and was informed I might find her residing here."

"Oh, yes, that is my Mama, step inside and I will tell her she has a visitor." Once he was in the hallway, she beckoned adding, "Come into the parlour—well it is not such really but the best place for you to wait. Would you care to take a seat?" As she faced him, she noticed that aside from him having pleasant features and being clean-shaven, he had a certain puzzled look on his face that she could not quite understand.

Without answering her question, he said, "So you are Gertrude's daughter, are you? Do you mind if I ask how old you are, my dear?" He now held his felt hat in his hand and gestured towards her with it, as he asked this question.

Faith stared up at him as he still stood just inside the door, wondering what that had to do with anything. The next fleeting thought was that he might be a man of the law or like seeking her mother for past misdemeanours. That thought fled just as swiftly, as she scoffed at herself for even thinking that her pious Ma could ever have done anything that would incur the wrath of the law. "I am looking forward to my seventeenth birthday within a week or two, but would you mind me asking why that would be of interest to you, sir?"

Before he had a chance to answer, her Ma appeared at the door, a cloth in her hands that she was using to dry them. She took one look at the stranger, muttered in a shocked whisper, "Bryce, is that you?" and collapsed in a heap on the floor.

Faith and this man who could be Bryce as she had called him, both fell to their knees at her side, and Faith patted her Ma's cheek as she pleaded with her to wake up. The stranger picked her up with care and lay her on the one sofa in the room. Bewildered, Faith stood by. Never in her life had she seen her Ma in any way incapable of standing on her own two feet. Now she was scared. If just seeing this man sent her into a faint, then he obviously was not a bearer of good news but something dire.

As her Mama opened her eyes and as swiftly as she had fainted sat up yanking at the hem of her skirt to ensure her ankles were covered, she demanded in an aggrieved tone, "What do you want, Bryce Witherton? How dare you turn up at my house without invitation or warning? Get out." With that order she pointed to the door, stood, shook the hand directed at him, and shouted, "Get out—now."

Chapter Two

"Can we not talk awhile like old friends, Gertrude?" he asked as he stepped back a pace or two and picked up the hat he had discarded.

"Old friends?" she shouted, so loud that Bertha appeared at the parlour door, looking distressed. Gert looked her way and ordered in a tone that could not be ignored, "Get back to your dishes."

As Bertha scampered out of the room, Faith looked up to the man who now seemed even taller as he stiffened his broad shoulders as he said, "Surely you have forgiven me after all these years, I was just as young and foolish as you, and had no part in your dismissal. Surely you realised that it was all down to my mother, and sadly she has passed on just six months ago."

A glimmer of the meaning of his visit began to dawn on Faith. Her Ma did not talk a lot about her past life but had told her years ago that she met Faith's Pa after she left the family that she originally came to the colonies with when she was a child of twelve. Her own parents perished after catching cholera and so she was picked out from an orphanage by the woman she then worked for—a woman it seems was this man's mother.

"Forgiven you?" Gert's voice now rose to almost a screech. "That, my good man is something I will never do." Suddenly remembering that Faith was still in the room, she waved a hand his way again, and repeated, "Get out and never return. There is no reason for you to disturb our lives again." She then walked to the door, opened it wide and pointed towards the passageway.

As he reached her at the door, he nodded in Faith's direction as he waved his hat towards her and said, "I would say, dear woman, that we have a very good reason to meet again." He sighed, twisted the hat around in his fingers and added, "My mother bequeathed me a substantial legacy—not exactly a fortune—but enough to see me live out my life in comfort, and as yet I have found no one who suits to share my life with. I am assuming this girl here who is approaching womanhood does not know the full story so I will leave that for you to discuss with her."

He went to walk out but then faced Gert again, saying softly, "I have a room at the Royal Hotel and intend to stay there for a while. Should you change your mind about sparing me a short few moments of your time, I await your presence eagerly." Faith trailed behind her Ma as she followed him to the door. He opened it and turned back to add, "I am happy that you seem to have made a good life for yourself and child Gertrude, but I am certain I could make life a lot easier for both of you should you change your mind."

"We are perfectly happy and contented with the life we have, and do not need your help or that of any man, thank you. Goodbye." She waved him through the door, slamming it shut as he cleared the step.

"Mama, just who was that man?" Faith dared to ask as they both went back to the kitchen where Bertha was donning her coat, about to go home to the house a short walk away that she shared with her son.

"Good night to you both," she said as she sent Faith a smile, before hurrying out.

Gertrude waited until the door closed behind her before saying to Faith, "Never you mind, my girl. No sense in denying that I knew him before I met your Pa, but why he should have the idea that I have a need to let him intrude on our lives I cannot fathom." She fussed about for a few minutes moving things that Bertha had already put in their correct place. "Turn down the lamp and let us get to our beds, girl. I am sorely worn after all the bother." Faith noticed that her Ma's cheeks were still flushed from the confrontation but knew too well that it was useless to ask more questions at this time.

Faith lay in her narrow cot and stared up at the dim ceiling. The man who rented the room above theirs stomped about for a few moments before the house went quiet. What the stranger Bryce had hinted at went around and around in her head. It seemed plain that her Ma was dismissed from the house she had called home for quite a few years, but just why? This Bryce was of similar age so must have been involved somehow in the dismissal. "Mama, why were you dismissed," she dared to ask, but was not surprised when she got no response. Her Ma was either asleep or feigning slumber.

Unlike other girls of her age, Faith had been well taught by her Ma, who told her that for a few years she had shared lessons with the son of the house. Lessons given by a tutor in the big house where she worked and that was why she was so well-versed in letters and numbers. It now seemed obvious that she likely shared the schooling with this man Bryce.

Thumping at her pillow, Faith turned over and tried to sleep, but slumber evaded her, and she lay for hours with thoughts going over and over in her brain. Despite her Ma's objections to the stranger, Faith felt strangely drawn to him. An emotion she found unsettling. One thing was certain; she sincerely hoped he would not give up his pursuit.

Her Ma was still a young woman in her prime, so why did she live her life as if it was almost over. The life she had made for them was surely a good one compared to some, but none the less was one of endless toil. If he could offer them a better life without this daily grind of cleaning and running after their lodgers, then why did her Ma not even consider it?

Murky light was creeping in through the tiny window when she opened her eyes. Her Ma's bed was empty. They usually rose at daybreak so that was not unusual. What was unusual was that her Ma had not given her a shake as she normally did. Faith climbed out of bed and shivered as she pulled her clothes on hastily and re-braided her hair. The spring days were brightening but the mornings could still be chilly.

Bertha was already in the kitchen when Faith went in to wash her hands and face in the tin basin of warmed water Bertha kindly left for her in the sink. "Morning dearie, your Ma's gone up top to see to the old duck up there." She jerked a thumb towards the ceiling. Their one current permanent guest was a woman of middle age who needed help in the mornings at times with her dressing due to her aches and pains. Usually, Ma sent Faith up there to perform this chore. "Did she say anything about the visitor after I left?" Bertha asked in a soft voice. "Quite a bit of excitement, eh?" She began to bring the crockery needed for breakfast from the cupboard.

"Not a word, Bertha, but you know my Ma." Faith shrugged. Bertha loved a gossip and Faith had a notion news of the stranger had more than likely already reached the ears of one or two of her fellow housekeepers, and if not already soon would be. "She will tell me more in her own time." Faith had her doubts about that claim. "He seemed very nice though, so perhaps he will return."

The old nameless fellow who came in every morning to empty the chamber pots and do other menial tasks to earn a few pence, interrupted their conversation. He seldom spoke except for muttering something that might have been a greeting or a complaint.

A rap on the front door signalled a delivery, and Faith waved a hand Bertha's way offering, "I'll answer, you get on with what you were doing." A fluttering in her belly signalled how she hoped it was Walt and not his father's other deliveryman.

As luck would have it, as she opened the door wide, Walt doffed his hat and said with a grin, "Good morning fair maiden, what a sight for sore eyes you are on this murky morning." As he replaced his hat, he

24

leaned closer to say low, "I was expecting dear old Bertha so it must be my lucky day."

Faith had no words for that as she put a hand to her cheek that she knew had turned rosy. He went back to his cart and began to lift down two sacks and a box. "Lead ahead fair Faith and I will follow," he said on a chuckle. Certain that he was teasing she did as he suggested. Once he had been assured by Bertha where to leave the groceries in the cool room off the kitchen, he sent a wink Faith's way as he asked, "Have you made plans yet for that big celebration?"

Faith realised that the appearance of the stranger had forced all thought of her birthday out of her mind. She trailed Walt as he headed back up the passage, and at that moment, her Ma came down the stairs, stopping to pass a few words with Walt about their delivery, so Faith stood by awkwardly, unsure whether or not she should flee back to the kitchen.

Bertha chose then to call out, "Come eat your porridge while it is hot," and so Walt simply nodded her way before going out.

As Faith went to close the door, feeling slightly disappointed that he hadn't dallied with her for a while longer, she noticed a small shaggy head peeking out from the back of the cart. "I did not know you had a dog," she said as she took a step towards the cart and then faltered, thinking he may think her too forward.

With a small shake of the head, he said, "Oh, it's not really mine; I saved him from a bad fate when some old codger was ill-treating the poor little tyke. After he told me to keep my nose out of his business, I offered him a few pence for the small creature, and he gladly passed him over." He lifted the small black and white dog from the cart and offered him to Faith. "Would you like him? Take him from me if you would. My Ma was not best pleased when I took him home as we already have two animals, and she feels that is enough for one household. They keep the rats away." He held the dog at arm's length and the creature whimpered.

Faith longed with all her heart to accept the dog, but said, "Oh, no, Ma would not let me keep an animal in the house. He is a fine-looking dog, though." That was not exactly true, as the small dog was far away from being fine, with scraggly hair and a face that could be termed by some as ugly.

Walt grinned. "I understand. He can keep me company on my rounds, and my Ma will not complain as long as he stays with me and does not enter the shop." He placed the small creature back in the cart, turned to her and added, "I will give him a wash and smarten him up." Pushing his hair back he tapped his forehead and said, "Well, I'd best be off."

Faith watched as he climbed onto his bench at the front of the cart, not failing to notice how agile he was, with strong legs and arms. But then she shook her head, wondering what on earth she was thinking of, admiring a boy's limbs. Hurriedly she closed the door.

"That is one very nice lad," Bertha said as she placed their bowls of porridge in front of them. "I think he has a fancy for you, young Faith." She tapped Faith on the shoulder.

"Stop your silly nonsense, woman and get on with your chores," her Ma chose to offer in a tone filled with disapproval. "Have you set the table in the dining room?"

Before Bertha scurried from the room, she sent Faith a wink and a shake of the head, ensuring her Ma could not see.

The day went along in the usual way, and not a word about the stranger and his visit passed her Ma's lips. Faith had become used to her Ma's long silences and came to realise over time that she just did not wish to disclose her past or anyone who had inhabited this past. It irked Faith that her Ma was so unlike other mothers she knew who shared laughter and fun moments with their daughters more so than their sons. Daisy Finch doted on her daughter Florrie and made it obvious how proud she was of the girl. Faith wondered why her own Ma had never done such, even when she was small, and others said how smart she was, and this hurt.

"Do you still have the notion to invite your friends over to celebrate your birthday with you?" her Ma asked a few days before the day, surprising Faith so much she stared at her as if struck dumb. "Though Lord knows why you should have such high and mighty ideas I do not know."

Trust Ma to add that last part, Faith thought as she said, "Well, only if you are agreeable Mama. It would just be Grace Barker and Florrie Finch." Biting her lip, she quickly added, "And perhaps Florrie's brother Walter might like to be invited. As Bertha said, he is a well-mannered young man. I am not too well acquainted with others of similar age." That was a fact, like so many other young folks in in the district, she was always too busy for socialising. Even when younger she had been working while others played at their childish games.

Her Ma's head went back as she digested that. Bertha chose to join in by saying, "What a splendid idea Missus, heaven knows the girl works hard and deserves something fancy for a change."

"Something fancy!" Faith's Ma glared at Bertha as if she had suggested they invite the Governor or Queen Victoria herself. "Don't get ideas above your station, madam. Just the friends you mentioned for tea in the afternoon. Perhaps you can make a nice cake Bertha, and a few delicacies as you suggested."

"Wonderful." Bertha clapped her chubby hands together. Gert walked out of the room without saying another word on the subject but Bertha in her excitement sat at the table and began to make her list. "Get along to the store and pick up some extras for me, Faith, and while there you can invite both Florrie and Walt, and then go along to invite young Grace. What time is best do you think? Not too close to lunch or dinner so perhaps make it four o clock, what do you say?"

"Thank you, Bertha." Faith bent to place a kiss on her rosy cheek. "What would I do without you?"

"Oh, get off with you and run along." She flapped her list as she waved her hand.

Faith retrieved her shawl from the bedroom and left the house, her step jaunty. It was so unlike her Ma to suggest this that she could not help but wonder if there might be another reason for her strange behaviour. As luck would have it as she neared the store Walter was on the road outside, in the process of loading the cart. Faith's heart beat a little faster and she felt tongue-tied as he looked up and a saucy grin split his face.

Doffing his cap, he said, "Well here is a pleasant surprise. Enough to brighten a dull old day." He leant against the side of his cart and stroked the pup, who then licked his hand.

"I have a special list." Faith swallowed as she realised how stupid that sounded. "I see you still have your friend. Have you given him a name yet?"

"Yes, he is going to be Bob." He turned to the cart and picked up the dog to place it on the ground. Looking up at Faith the dog sat and lifted a paw. "Bob is very smart, and well mannered, see he is offering a paw for you to shake." That was accompanied by a laugh.

"Oh." She bent and took the offered paw. The dog licked her hand, and she withdrew it. "What else does he do?"

"Give him time. Between my jobs and lifting and moving loads, I have little time for training. See the end of his tail. It's what Florrie called a bobble, so that's how he got the name."

"Ah yes, she is correct." Faith then stood, feeling rather silly for she was so unused to such friendly chat that she did not know what else to say. Remembering the reason for her visit to the store she held the list aloft saying, "I had best get on with my shopping." As she turned to enter the store she said, "I am having afternoon tea on my birthday. As it was your suggestion that I celebrate, would you care to join us? I am about to ask Florrie if she will come, and Bertha said that perhaps I should ask you." Shifting from foot to foot, she added hastily, "But maybe you have better things to do. I will be asking Grace Barker so no doubt you would not wish to be surrounded by us silly girls."

He obviously thought that funny for his grin was wide as he said, bowing slightly, "I would be honoured to attend. I feel obligated somehow, seeing as I was the one who suggested it. Nothing pleases me more than being in the company of young ladies. I find them much more interesting than males of my own age—silly oafs, always talking nonsense and indulging in rollicking and stupid behaviour."

Certain he was now teasing her for sure, she just nodded and went hurriedly into the store. Florrie and her ma were serving, and Florrie was delighted with the invitation. When Faith went back outside Walt and his cart were gone. Step light, she then went on to invite Grace.

Later that afternoon, after dinner had been served to the guests and Faith and her Ma sat at the table while Bertha set the remaining beef, potatoes, and cabbage onto their three plates, Bertha asked, "Have you a notion what you intend to do with your guests, Faith dear?"

Faith shrugged. "Not a notion in the world, Bertha. What do you suggest? Your son has a boy does he not? How did they celebrate his last birthday?"

Bertha sat and picked up her knife and fork as she thought that over. "I do recall they had some fun with a game of sorts where they tossed hoops of rope onto a wooden peg." She thought some more and then added, "Ah yes, he said it was called quoits. Shall I fetch that along? It is also a game that the grown-ups play it seems—so your guests should be amused. And you should have some music. Old Mister Sims who sells his wares around the diggings has an instrument, and he likes to play it, so what about I ask him if he could spare the time. All he would expect is a nice slice of cake and a glass of ale, I am sure."

Faith looked over to Gert, but she said nothing, so Faith said, "That would be lovely, Bertha, thank you. Is Mister Sims a particular friend of yours? I have seen you chatting to him now and then."

She didn't miss the slight blush that tinged Bertha's already rosy cheeks as she waved a hand her way. "We do pass the time of day I must admit. I think he is lonely. He has no kin that I know of. It's not much of a life travelling from one dig to another and listening to the woes of the miners. I have made a small purchase from him now and then."

No more was said about the celebration, and to Faith's surprise and pleasure her Ma came into the bedroom the night before the party with something over her arm. She held a pretty frock aloft saying, "I wore this when I first met your Pa, so perhaps you can wear it tomorrow. It's not too fancy mind, and certainly not the latest fashion, but better than your shabby old day clothes."

"It's beautiful Ma." Faith took the garment and shook it out. Made of a soft fabric of blue with a pattern of small buds adorning it, the skirt had two flounces. The bodice was unadorned, with puffy sleeves such as Faith had seen in one of the newspapers advertising the current dress trends in London. "Can I try it on to ensure it fits?"

"You can be sure it will fit, as you are about the same in size and height as I was years ago."

"I didn't know you owned anything so pretty, Ma." That was a fact. They only ever wore their simple black everyday skirts and blouses.

"I forgot I owned it, girl. It must have been pushed to the bottom of my trunk. Try it on if you must. I am weary and ready for my bed." With that she went out with a lantern and Faith heard the back door close behind her as she visited the outhouse they were lucky enough to now have at the end of the small yard where they grew a variety of vegetables.

Quickly Faith stripped off her skirt and blouse, both of which had seen better days, and pulled the dress over her head. As they had no mirror large enough for her to see how she looked, nevertheless the soft fabric felt wonderful beneath her work worn hands and yes, it fit perfectly and was just the right length. How she wished she possessed nice underthings and a pair of shoes other than the plain black pumps or the ankle boots that were the only footwear she possessed. Even so, she thought how lucky she was that her Ma had a change of heart and not only gave permission for her celebration but also found this treasure for her to wear. She danced a small jig in the small space allowed between the beds.

Before sleep claimed her, Faith wondered if Walt would find her pretty in the dress.

* * *

"Please help yourselves to more of Bertha's splendid fruit cake or the small pies she made," Faith offered her three guests. Apart from the main dining table, the room also held two small round tables and the four of them sat at one of these beneath the window that faced the street. To her dismay both Florrie and Grace had

34

arrived attired in frocks far more up to date and pretty than her own.

Walt had been his usual well-mannered self, bowing to her Ma, but had not seemed to notice Faith's new dress. As she was not acquainted with the likes and dislikes of men, she had no idea if that was normal. He did offer her a lovely posy of wildflowers as he came in and to Faith that was the best gift she had ever or would ever receive. Florrie handed her a small bag of fruit drops, and Grace presented her with spiced nuts.

Bertha had insisted that Faith not wear her hair in its usual braid but had pulled back the sides and secured her well-brushed locks behind her head with a bow that matched the blue of the frock. Faith rarely wore her hair loose and it felt strange, but at least she did not feel out of place as both her friends had theirs left to hang down their backs. Faith was thankful that once the guests had arrived, her Ma disappeared, saying she had work to attend to. Once Bertha had ensured they all had refreshments, that Walt's posy sat centre table, and all else was to her liking she also went back to her kitchen.

"Your cook is certainly talented," Grace said as she helped herself to another pie— her third. "Our kitchen staff are not so good. My Mama is always complaining about them." Her small nose wrinkled as she spooned more custard on her pie.

Walt, who sat on Faith's right, said, "Our Ma likes to cook so she takes care of all that herself. Mind you, she does not have paying guests to worry about as you do, Faith."

Faith wasn't quite sure if he was hinting that his Ma and Pa didn't need to take in lodgers as they were wealthy enough. She felt more tongue-tied than usual in his company. Apart from greeting them and thanking them all for their gifts when they arrived together, she had mostly remained silent. Feeling it was time for her to say something, she blurted, "Mister Sims has agreed to come and play some music for us after we have finished eating."

"Oh, is that the old fellow who hawks his goods around the diggings," Grace said. "I hope he takes the trouble to bathe. Last time he walked near me in the street, he stunk as if he had lingered where the night man dumps the nightsoil."

"The poor old soul has nowhere to call home, Grace, so we should be more charitable," Walt chided. "Not all of us are lucky enough to have decent beds to sleep in and someone there to pander to our needs."

Grace looked noticeably chastised by his remark and took another pie. Faith felt a warm glow that Walt had defended someone less fortunate than himself. Once most of the food had been eaten and Bertha returned to inquire if they needed any more fruit juice, Walt said, "Shall we play the game Bertha mentioned she had left for us?" Earlier Bertha had brought the quoits in and explained how to use it, and Walt had exclaimed that he thought it would be fun.

After moving the table back so that they had more room the game kept them occupied for an hour. By the time Bertha announced that Mister Sims had arrived they were having so much fun that Faith was reluctant to end it—pleased that she appeared to be more skilful than the other two girls at getting the ring over the post. Twice Walt had congratulated her, which did not appear to please Grace.

"At least the old fellow has cleaned up a fraction," Grace commented to Florrie behind a hand in a half whisper. Faith decided she did not like the spoilt girl all that much. Either Walt did not hear her this time or chose to ignore her, but he said nothing as he packed the game away in its bag.

"Let us move to the parlour," Faith said as she gestured before her, and they all trooped into the small room adjacent to the dining room.

To Faith's surprise, Mister Sims was very skilled on his small, strange instrument, that he called a squeezebox, and began to play a lively polka. Bertha joined them after tidying the dining room, and she began to clap her hands along with the music. "He plays to the diggers sometimes, so he told me," she whispered to Faith. "I expect that's why he is good at it."

The best part of the afternoon came when Walt extended a hand to Faith, asking, "Would the birthday girl care to dance with me—mind you, you'd best watch out for your dainty feet as I am not too good at this cavorting thing."

Faith took his offered hand, which was warm and noticeably strong. "I must confess I have never done such a dance either so it is likely your feet that will need to be careful of mine."

He chuckled at that, and they began to do what she could only consider a sort of jumping up and down and swinging round. In her enjoyment, she laughed aloud as he held his arm aloft and guided her beneath it. When old Sim's music stopped after reaching a crescendo, Faith was breathless as she sank onto a chair.

"That's called a polka," Bertha explained, as she patted Faith's knee. "Play another one Sims," she called out and after taking a swig of the beer she had left at his side, he started again, this time playing a softer tune similar to a lullaby. This brought back a vivid memory from Faith's childhood, and she suddenly recalled that her Ma would sing something similar to her when she was still barely walking. Why had Ma stopped singing? Faith seemed to recall that she had a beautiful voice, as she lulled her to sleep.

Grace came to stand in front of Walt, holding her hand palm up in front of him. "Come dance with me, Walter," she said in a demanding tone, and then looked annoyed when he did not take the outstretched hand.

"A lady does not ask such of a man," Bertha admonished which seemed to annoy Grace even more. With a flounce of her skirts, she went to plonk herself down on the chair, mumbling something that only Florrie could hear. Turning to Faith, Bertha said low, "That one needs to be taught some manners."

Faith agreed with her and now wished she had not invited Grace. But her choices were few, as she had no other friends of her own age. That thought saddened her. Old Sam played another polka and when Walt asked his sister to dance with him, the glare Grace sent his way should have sent him afire. He did not seem to notice—or ignored it, which pleased Faith no end.

Faith's Ma came in then. With a look around the room, she said, "Bertha, time you were preparing the evening meal."

Rubbing her hands together she added, "Faith say goodbye to your company." Her glance at Mister Sims should have turned him to stone as she sniffed and waved him on his way.

As Faith said farewell to Grace, Florrie, and Walt, she caught sight of a figure striding along on the far side of the road, a man she recalled from his recent visit. Her Ma had not mentioned Bryce Witherton once since that evening and Faith wondered if he was heading their way or simply taking a stroll. A beggar woman stopped him, saying something that was likely a plea for money, and he delved into his pocket and handed her a coin before walking on.

Grace barely muttered a thank you or farewell before marching briskly in the opposite direction to Florrie. About to follow his sister, Walt turned back. "Thank you for a most enjoyable afternoon," he said with a smile. "I neglected to tell you how pleasant you look in your nice frock." He fingered a lock of her hair that had fallen over her shoulder. "I like your hair down like that. You should wear it that way more often, it is beautiful."

Faith knew her cheeks had reddened, and her tongue seemed to have stuck to the roof of her mouth. Barely had she time to nod and say a soft, "Thank you," than he had given her a carefree wave and strode after his sister. "And thank you for the flowers," she called, but he continued walking, so she was unsure if he heard.

He had left her in such a bemused condition that she had not noticed Mr. Witherton cross the road. "Good afternoon—or should I say evening, to you, Faith. I hope I have not intruded on what was obviously a visit with friends. I was in the vicinity of your home and dared pay your good mother another call, merely to ascertain if she had changed her way of looking at things since my last intrusion in your lives."

Faith rubbed at her cheek. What should she say to him? Should she tell him that not once had her Ma mentioned him or his odd evening call? "Ma will be busy in the kitchen helping our cook prepare for the evening meal." That sounded offensive to her so she quickly added, "Please come into the parlour and I will fetch her. Perhaps you would care to dine with us." Biting her lip at that offer, she wondered if her Ma would be angry with her for being so forward.

He seemed pleased at that, and stepped into the hallway, removing his hat. "That would be a pleasure, but if this is not a good time, perhaps I should leave it until another day."

"I will ask Mama, so take a seat and she will be with you soon." Faith gestured to the worn old sofa, and he sat, his hat held in his hands.

"Can I take that?" Faith reached out and took it from him, but then was not sure where to put it so lay it on the one small side table.

"I saw your visitors leaving. Were you celebrating your anniversary? I recall you said you were nearing your seventeenth birthday. Was it today?"

Faith stared at him as her chin tucked in. How did this stranger remember such a small item from their conversation that did not last long before her Ma intervened and told him to leave? "Yes." Her response sounded rather short, but he had taken her by complete surprise.

"Then, I hope it has been a happy one."

Before she could reply to that, her Ma came bursting into the room, looking very dishevelled. "I did not know we had a visitor," she said, not sounding at all pleased.

Mr. Witherton stood abruptly and held out a hand. "I do apologise, I seem to have come at a very inappropriate time. Perhaps I should return at a more suitable date."

"No need for that. I made it clear—or so I thought—that we had nothing to discuss." Gert turned to face Faith, waved a hand her way and said in what Faith heard as a distinctly harassed tone, "Go assist Bertha, girl."

Faith looked from her to the man and went out of the room at an almost run. Barely had the door closed behind her than she heard her Ma shout, "For heaven's sake, I thought I made it clear to you on your last call, you are not welcome here and I do not wish to discuss our past with you. Get out of my house and do not come back."

Bertha grimaced towards Faith when she entered the kitchen. "What on earth has got into your Mama, Faith? I have never heard her in such a tizzy before."

Faith shrugged her shoulders and slumped onto a chair.

Chapter Three

"I invited the gentleman to share our meal with us," Faith said, now feeling that she would earn the wrath of her Ma's tongue later. "Did she mention the visitor at all to you or his reason for turning up at our door?"

Bertha spread her hands and shook her head. "Never a word. But your Ma is not one to confide in anyone, especially in me. I thought she might have discussed the stranger with you, seeing as he seemed to have shared a part of her life with her before you were born."

"My Ma has secrets it seems. Perhaps I will learn more now." Faith went to the door. "He is still in there, so she has not thrown him out. Prepare another place for him at the table, Bertha, just in case he does persuade her to allow him to stay this time."

About to turn back, Faith heard the man say, "Your daughter has reached marriageable age, Gertrude, and is no longer a child to be fobbed off with lies. Do you not think that she has a right to learn the truth about her birth?" Shocked to her bones, Faith stood there in a daze.

After his last visit she was left to wonder about the part this gent took in her Ma's dismissal, which seemed to have somehow involved him. That statement made her now feel that her birth was not as simple as her Ma had always explained it. What did he mean by the truth about her birth? Was that the big secret? Had her Ma lied all Faith's life about the truth of her parent? The man she had called Papa was different in every way to Faith, with a swarthy skin, and hair that was almost red in shade, and he was a very tall man.

In fact, Faith recalled that when about six she had asked him why she did not have the same colour hair. "Don't always work out that way, child," was his response. "You favour your Ma's looks and colour. Wouldn't want to look like an old cabbage faced sod like me now, would you?" At the time, in her childish innocence, she had taken his words as the truth. "And my skin is darker than yours through many hours working out in the midday sun."

Going to sit at the table, Faith put her head in her hands and realised that her face was damp with tears. "I do not understand this, Bertha," she wailed. "What has this man to do with my birth?"

Bertha sat at her side and put her arms about Faith. "Don't fret my dear one, surely your Ma will now explain what this is all about to you."

Faith had a feeling her Ma was not likely to ever do that. She made to rise and at that moment her Ma's voice clearly rang out as she shouted, "Keep out of our lives from now on Bryce Witherton, and do not come here again stirring up the past along with all the strife you put me through. We are managing fine my girl and I, and do not wish to have someone such as you come along and dig up happenings that brought such pain. It all happened so many years ago, so Lord knows what you are thinking to do by coming back here."

Bertha and Faith exchanged a glance as the front door slammed. Gert did not come into the kitchen but went along the passage and they heard her go through the back door into the yard, likely on her way to the outhouse. "Best get the food moving," Bertha said as she stirred the pot on the stovetop vigorously. "The guests will be expecting their meal soon. I heard old Madam Pollock coming downstairs. Never misses a meal that one."

Later, when Faith took Mrs. Pollock's meal into the dining room, to her surprise the old woman asked, "How did your birthday celebration go, my dear?" Without waiting for a response, she handed Faith a small cloth bag, which she took from the pocket of her skirt. "Here's a small trinket for you. It is not newly purchased, but I have no need for such frivolous fancy

46

things these days and thought you might like it now that you are of an age to wear such ornaments."

"Why, thank you, Madam," Faith said with pleasure as she drew a brooch from the small sachet. It contained blue gemstones set in the pattern of a rose, which caught the light from the lamp that made it glitter as Faith moved it around on her palm. "It is beautiful—I have never received such a lovely gift. Did you wear this when you were my age?"

With a wave of a veined and misshapen hand she said, "Bless you no. My husband brought that for me on our wedding day." Sighing, she seemed sad for a moment, but then brightened. "We both worked in a big house in Melbourne, I as downstairs maid and he in the stables tending to the horses that he loved."

"I will cherish this gift, thank you again." As Faith put it into the pocket of her skirt she wondered just when she would have a chance to wear such a splendid piece of jewelry.

"Ensure you do wear it, Faith dear. In my view you spend far too much time around here." With a wave of the hand, she encompassed the room and house as a whole. Taking Faith's hand, she pulled her closer and added in a conspiratorial tone, "It is always good to have something you can barter with my dear, for you never know what travails life will bring you."

Not knowing what to say to that small piece of sage advice, Faith smiled down at the kindly woman. As she went to see if the other lodgers required anything more, it occurred to her that the gift might be of some value. As she was about to go back to the kitchen Mrs. Pollock beckoned her over again. Looking secretive, she leant close and said in a soft voice so no one else could hear, "I could hear raised voices earlier. Is everything all right with your mother, my dear?"

Taken aback, Faith shook her head. "Why yes, I think she was simply not happy with one of her visitors. I have no idea what happened, but you can be sure my Ma will be fine. As you know she is a woman who does not let mere trifles worry her." Faith hoped that explanation would satisfy the woman.

Sadly, it did not. With a small harrumph, she said, "I saw the gent as he walked across the street, and he seemed intent on his mission as he strode towards here. A fine-looking man if ever I saw one."

Faith sucked her bottom lip in as she pondered on an answer to that, and at that moment her Ma poked her head around the door and called out, "Faith, Bertha needs you in the kitchen." With a nod at Madam Pollock Faith hurried out.

Her Ma's mood and manner did not falter as she ate her meal. Stern faced and tight lipped she stared at Faith as, after growing tired of the silence between them, she asked, "Did Mr. Witherton upset you Ma?"

That question seemed to annoy her, which Faith found odd. "Upset me? What gave you that notion?"

Bertha and Faith exchanged a look of confusion. It seemed her mother was going to carry on as if the earlier incident was commonplace. "Mrs. Pollock gave me a gift." Faith pulled out the small bag and withdrew its contents, which she fingered lovingly.

"What in heaven's name is the silly old fool giving you such trinkets for? You should return it."

Faith stared at her before spluttering, "Why would I return such a gift? It is the loveliest thing I have ever seen, and I will treasure it always." Holding the brooch close to her breast, she shook her head.

Her Ma jumped out of her chair, came around the table and gripped Faith's arm, pulling her up. "Come, I will tell her you cannot accept it."

"But..." Faith reeled back and dug in her heels. Used to her Ma's cold manner and stern ways, she nonetheless was shocked by the fierce look in her Ma's eyes. "I will not insult a person who thought of me so kindly. Why on earth should I not keep such a gift?"

"Because I do not trust such gift givers. Next you know she will be expecting more from you."

With a puzzled frown, Faith shook her head in total confusion. Knowing that she was ignorant of the ways of the larger world, she still could not see why accepting a gift could in any way put her in debt to the giver. Determined not to give in to her Ma this time, she sat again, pushed the brooch back into its pouch, and into her pocket.

Without another word, her Ma turned and marched from the room, going straight to the dining room. Faith followed her but went no further than the door. Mrs. Pollock was in the middle of folding her serviette, which she did with extreme care once she caught sight of Gert. Holding her breath, Faith waited for her Ma to say something that might be just about the worst thing she could ever utter.

"I would like to have a word with you in private," was what she did say as she nodded to Mrs. Pollock. "Let us go to the parlour." The other diners, all men, watched the pair of women as they left the room. Bertha gave Faith a look of inquiry before going to collect the used dishes.

Her Ma made no objections when Faith followed them to the parlour where Mrs. Pollock sat on the sofa with a sigh. "I presume you are not happy with my gift to your daughter, and before you begin to harangue me, let me tell you why I gave it to her."

"I do not trust gift-givers, and that is the truth. My daughter does not need your trinket or advice, thank you." That last was added without a trace of gratitude but more as an insult.

"So she is to go through life without receiving a small piece of kindness from anyone, is that it? The girl works all hours in this godforsaken house, without a kind word from you, her mother, and so now you begrudge her receiving what is simply a small trinket in appreciation for all the help and kindness she has shown me since coming here. Heaven knows everyone gets little in the way of appreciation from you, madam."

Faith watched as colour flooded her Ma's cheeks. Seeming to be lost for words, her mouth twisted, and Faith felt that at any moment steam might come out of her ears. "It is no business of yours, Madam, how I treat my daughter. In addition, I would thank you to keep your stuck up nose out of our affairs. Furthermore, you can find yourself other lodgings as you are no longer welcome in this house." With what seemed to Faith to be a flounce she turned, brushed past Faith, and went to their bedroom where she slammed the door.

Mrs. Pollock let out a heavy sigh as she signalled for Faith to come closer. "I would never have given the gift if I thought for one moment it would cause such a disaster." With hands on knees, she pushed herself up and said in a soft tone, "It is my belief that your mother grew bitter after it was clear that she was with child, that child being you Faith dear girl." Pausing she looked past Faith to ensure they were alone before continuing. "I did not know her well as such, but knew of her, as I went to work in the big house about the time the scandal blew up."

"Scandal? I do not understand." Faith shook her head, feeling as if she was drifting in a fog. "Ma left the big house, or so it was told to me, when she met my Papa, and he was the one who aided her when she was alone and friendless in Melbourne. He later, some time after their wedding, insisted they come to Ballarat in search of gold as so many others were doing."

"I have likely said too much, Faith dear girl. I do not wish to cause you pain. Heaven knows you have had a hard time of it with that harridan of a woman who seems to think the entire world is against her." With another huge sigh, she turned for the door, and with a hand on Faith's arm said, "I will now search for new lodgings, and perhaps we can meet up again once I get settled there, and I will tell you all that I know."

"No, do not go, Madam, for I am certain my Ma will relent and allow you to stay." Everything she had said so far had just mystified Faith more. Her belief was that Mrs. Pollock came to the town with her husband and he died before he could stake his claim. Could she really know more about her Ma, and what happened all those years ago? A sudden thought hit her—how strange it seemed that all this had come out to add to the mysterious appearance in their lives of Bryce Witherton.

"No, Faith dear, I would prefer to find more suitable lodgings, in fact it has been my thought for some time to return to Melbourne. That is what I will probably do, but as soon as I am settled for now, I would like you to call on me, away from this house and your mother's rule. How does that sound?"

"Well, I would much prefer it if you stayed, but if it is your decision to go then I would most certainly like to visit you. And thank you once again for my beautiful gift, I will always treasure it."

"One more thing. I must make it clear that the brooch is no mere bauble. It would fetch a tidy sum if you are ever in dire straits and need funds."

"You mean…mean, it is valuable?" Faith swallowed a lump that formed in her throat. Why was this woman, a person she barely knew, being so generous? "I don't understand."

As if suddenly in a hurry, she patted Faith on the arm and left the room. Faith sat on the sofa and took the small sachet from her pocket. Touching the brooch, tears filled her eyes. Apart from Bertha, no one had ever treated her so kindly. Was she forever to suffer the tantrums and dictates of her Ma? Never had the urge to get away been so strong. However, up until now the thought of leaving all that was familiar to her and going elsewhere seemed impossible. But if Mrs. Pollock was being truthful and the brooch was valuable perhaps there was a chance to get away? But where would she go, and would she have enough courage to defy her Ma?

Two days later Mrs. Pollock said her goodbyes to Faith and Bertha and with board straight back nodded to Gert before marching from the house. A man had come to collect her one trunk to transport it to her new chosen lodgings. Ensuring that Gert did not see, she surreptitiously handed Faith a scrap of paper with the details of her new chosen abode. Faith scurried out to the outhouse and was shocked when she read the scrawling writing; for Mrs. Pollock had chosen the same hotel that Bryce Witherton had told her Ma he was staying while in town.

"I miss the dear old thing," Bertha said later the same day. "She was no trouble, in fact least trouble than the men we get passing through." She plonked a dish on the table to show her disgust. "What was your Ma thinking? To toss a grand old person like her out for something so trifling." Wagging her wooden spoon at Faith, she said in a hushed voice, "Don't you ever let your Ma take that brooch away from you. I agree with Mrs. Pollock, there could come a day when it might come in handy. My advice is to secrete it somewhere your Ma is not likely to find it. Don't end up being a slave for anyone, Faith dear. You make your own decisions on your future. I have a feeling things are about to change around here." With that sage prediction, she disappeared into the larder and began to hum low as she sorted through her neatly stored packages and containers.

Faith's head was a whirl of thoughts. Suddenly all that was familiar to her seemed to be changing. What on earth was she to do with the brooch? Sadly, she agreed deep down with Bertha, feeling her Ma would find a way to take the gift away from her. For the first time ever, she felt something not quite nice about her Ma. Afraid to let the feeling surface, she pushed it further to the back of her mind.

* * *

"I saw your lodger, Mrs. Pollock, outside the hotel in deep conversation with that gent who visited your Ma a while back," Walt said as he lifted a sack of flour off the back of his cart.

Faith unbent from stroking Bob's soft ears. The pup was now allowed to run beside the cart when Walt made his deliveries. A week had passed since the drama of Mrs. Pollock changing lodgings and Faith had not yet found the courage or right time to visit the generous lady. Her Ma seemed to be watching her every move, which was as distressing as it was disturbing. Never had she felt like a prisoner in her home.

"Oh, I guess that is not so surprising seeing as they both rent accommodation there."

Walt set the sack down beside them and pushed his cap back as he shook his head. "'Twas a surprise to everyone that the dear lady moved. My Ma said she thought the woman was settled at your lodgings."

Faith shrugged, unsure how much to divulge of the occurrences that brought about the change. Could she trust Walt? It was a fact that he knew just about everything that went on in town, and she had no idea if he gossiped but guessed that folk passed the time of day with him. "I guess she simply wanted a change of surroundings." Faith hoped that explanation would settle it. It still surprised her that the lady could afford to lodge in such a fine hotel that would surely cost more than the twenty-seven shillings a week she paid for board at their lodgings.

Walt looked hard at her before lifting the sack again and going inside the house. Faith stayed where she was, glad to be out in the sunshine. "You are a very good boy," she told Bob who wagged his tail fiercely. How she wished her Ma would allow her to have a dog of her own. Walt came back out, whistling a merry tune as he returned to his cart. About to climb aboard, he turned back and for a moment seemed uncertain as he straightened his cap that was already perfectly set on his head. When he asked, "Would you care to take a ride with me when next I get an afternoon off, Faith?" So surprised was she that she simply stared at him in silence.

Truth was that she would like nothing more but had no idea what her Ma would say to that idea. Casting doubts aside, she said, "That would be nice, Walt. What day would that be?"

A grin split his face as he rubbed his ear, suddenly seeming to be stuck for words. "Perhaps Sunday...if that day suits you." Nibbling the end of his thumb, he added, "Would you like me to ask your Ma if she is agreeable?"

That was the last thing she wanted. Shaking her head, she nonetheless wondered how she could tell her Ma. "No, no Walt, that won't be necessary. What time?"

"Does about two o clock sound a good time?" His usual bravado seemed to have deserted him and Faith had the notion that he was feeling as nervous as she felt herself.

"That sounds like a perfectly suitable time."

With a nod, he said, "Sunday at two it is then." He then climbed aboard, whistled to Bob, touched his cap, and urged his horse forward.

Faith stood watching well after his cart was out of sight, her insides churning with a feeling such as she had never known before. On the one hand, excitement made her feel slightly sick and on the other hand, fear at what her Ma would say made her tremble. An idea struck; she would say that she was visiting Walt's sister Florrie. Her Ma could put up no objection to that. Seldom did she venture out herself so the likelihood of her seeing Faith with Walt was so slight it was not worth the worry of it. But nonetheless she did worry.

Later while she helped Bertha to set the tables for the evening meal she said in a whisper, "Walt has asked me to go for a ride with him on Sunday, Bertha, should I ask Ma?"

Bertha seemed pleased but then shook her head. "Dear me no, you go along dear, and I will do my best to keep your Ma here. I usually have Sunday afternoon to myself but have changed it to Saturday this week as my son is holding a small celebration and wants me to help him with it." Patting Faith on the arm she added, "Tell her you are meeting one of your friends, Florrie—or that other little stuck up one, what's her name, Grace Barker."

"That was my idea. I really do not like telling fibs, but feel it is the only way."

Bertha nodded sagely, leaning close to ask, "Would you like me to get your brooch from its hiding place for you to wear?" The brooch had been well and truly secured somewhere in the pantry—and Faith had no idea where—which was probably the best idea. Her Ma had a way of wheedling the truth out of her. Faith felt that her Ma had already made a thorough search through her own meagre belongings.

About to refuse, Faith said, "Maybe I will take it along with me, Bertha. Do you think I can trust Walt enough to disclose the truth of it?"

"My goodness me yes, I cannot think of another young man who is more trustworthy. And he surely has a soft spot for you, Faith dear." About to turn about she added softly, "He knows lots of people in all walks of trade around the town. Mayhap he can offer you sage advice on where to take it should you ever need to know its value."

Sound advice indeed. Deep down, Faith had a feeling that had stayed with her since taking possession of the gift, that Mrs. Pollock's reason for giving her the brooch was more to do with its value than its beauty. For it was obvious that an occasion for her to wear such a piece of jewelry was not likely to crop up in the foreseeable future.

The following two days passed in a haze of excitement as Faith pondered on what to wear. Not that she had a lot of choice. If she wore the dress her Ma presented her with to wear to her birthday celebration her Ma's suspicions would immediately be roused. So, she would need to select the best of her workday clothes, of which there was little choice.

As they ate their midday meal on Sunday, Faith said, "Florrie Finch has kindly asked me to visit, Ma. It is such a nice day that I thought to take a walk over there." She glanced at Bertha and swore she received a wink from her. Earlier Bertha had schooled her in what to say. It occurred to Faith to wonder how many other girls had to invent stories for their Mamas simply to spend time with a boy who showed them attention.

Gert's head went back as she stared at Faith and for one moment Faith held her breath, fearing that she was about to receive a scolding. To her surprise her Ma said, "As Bertha is here today, I suppose it won't hurt for you to go out. But don't dilly-dally there for long, mind you. We will still need your help at dinner now we have three extra lodgers to cope with."

"For certain Mama, I will be out no longer than an hour or two. I will be back well in time for dinner." Inside Faith wanted to shout and sing for joy at the ease with which the lie had been received.

Chapter Four

Faith fidgeted with her bonnet, then her hand went to the pocket of her skirt where the brooch was safely tucked. Determined that her Ma would not see her getting onto Walt's cart, she had walked a distance up the road, safe in the knowledge that Bertha would do her best to keep her Ma occupied for an hour or two with doing a thorough survey of their rations in the pantry.

When Bob came running to her as Walt's cart appeared, the butterflies that had inhabited her stomach since early morning turned to full-blown nerves and her hand shook as she stroked the dog's ear. As Walt pulled the horse to a stop, he saluted her before climbing down. "Well, here's a nice surprise. I thought you would be waiting at home."

"I was ready early and as it is such a nice sunny afternoon I thought I would stroll along to meet you," she lied, sure that he would guess the real reason.

"It is a pleasant afternoon, isn't it? Where would you like to go on this fine day?" He bent to lift Bob up to place him in the back of the cart and then offered a hand to assist Faith onto the bench seat. "Thought Bob would be safer up here with us as we might be going a bit faster than usual," he explained as Faith straightened her bonnet and then her skirt.

"Good idea. I have no idea where to go, Walt, I will leave the choice to you as I seldom go further than the main street to be honest." Faith thought a while as he clicked the horse into a slow trot, then added, "I would like to see the diggings, perhaps at Bowden that I have heard lodgers talking about. Oh, and could we go past the site of the stockade?"

"Your wish is my command, madam. Good choice." He sent a grin her way.

Faith's heart felt so light she thought it might fly from her chest. In all her years she had never shared a drive with a young man, and the thrill of sitting beside Walt made her want to shout for joy. It did not take long to reach the place where what was called the Eureka Stockade took place. Nobody would believe that a battle occurred there, as it now seemed a peaceful spot. "It is hard to believe that so many men died that awful night. I heard that one of your uncles was involved in the fight."

"Yes, that's a fact. He was severely injured." Walt heaved a heavy sigh. "'Twas almost six years to the day and he has never recovered. Still mines in the hope of striking it rich. Was your Pa involved in the battle?"

"No. We came up here from Melbourne and I think he had ideas of finding gold, but then decided to open the lodging house." Faith gazed at the trees waving in a slight breeze. "My Ma does not talk about him now, but I do have memories of their arguments because she considered him too lazy to try his hand at digging. Did you ever meet Peter Lalor, the man who organised it all?"

"No, but my uncle has spoken of his regard for the man. Shall we continue with our ride?"

"Of course." Faith settled back after reaching behind her to pat Bob. "He has grown a little since you first got him. Do you think he will get much bigger?" she asked, simply for something to say to hide her foolish nervousness.

"Who knows? As I have no idea of his parentage, it is a waiting game." Walt sent a grin her way. "I am so glad you agreed to this outing, Faith. What did your Ma say when you told her?"

Faith swallowed. Should she tell him the truth of the matter? "I told her I was visiting Florrie," she blurted as her cheeks flamed. "My Ma has some funny ideas, and I was not sure how she would react if I told her I was spending time with you."

Not sure if his chuckle meant that he thought her stupid or not she remained silent until he said, "That there is the quartz crushing battery." He pointed to the collection of small structures that had been erected a few years earlier. "If we continue to the top of the hill, you can see the digs and the river below, and we will stop to stretch our legs." Saying that, he continued upwards following the path. Once or twice, he sent a wave to a miner who was either working or sharing a drink with someone.

"It's a hard life, is it not? Do many of them make a fortune?" she asked, holding onto her bonnet that threatened to blow away, for the wind grew stronger as they climbed higher.

"I don't suppose they would let on if they did. We hear stories of the ones who make it and end up wealthy, but they keep it close to their chest. Whoa, Matilda," he pulled the horse up for they had reached the peak of the hill. "Shall we rest here awhile? Bob would like a run." Glancing about, he added, "and there's a patch of grass for my girl to pick at."

Faith was still smiling at the name he had given his mare, which she found endearing. "That would be nice." She waited until he came around to hand her down. As he placed her on the ground, it seemed he held her around the waist for longer than he needed to. This brought their faces to within an inch or two of each other and Faith licked her lips as she stared up at him, wondering if she imagined the small groan that left his lips before he released her.

Going to the cart, he assisted Bob down and then brought a blanket, which he spread out on the ground near a spindly windswept tree. "Ma thoughtfully sent us some lemon cordial and biscuits. Would you like some?"

"Yes, thank you. That was very thoughtful of her indeed." Faith swallowed at that for it sounded very formal. "Where did you pick the name for your horse?" she asked, as she stroked the mare's smooth neck.

With a small chuckle he put a finger to his nose as he said in a hush, "'Twas the name of one of my Pa's favourite customers. The old biddy would come into the shop and um and ah for half an hour over her choice of some silly thing. Pa jokingly said she had a thing for him. Sadly, she left this world when all alone one harsh winter's night."

"That is sad. It is not nice to be alone in the world, is it?"

"No, it is not, and that's a fact. Come sit," he beckoned for her to where he had set a small basket down on the blanket. Once they were settled and both held a cup of cordial and a biscuit, he said, "I ran into

Mrs. Pollock again yesterday, and she asked after you. Wanted to know if you were going all right. Said she was hoping you would visit her. Now, that is another poor lady that I fear is lonely."

"Oh. I have not had time yet, but I will go along there. Is she well? I like her very much."

"She seems to be fine. She did mention that she is thinking of either going back to Melbourne or maybe Geelong. I think life holds nothing for her up here any more without her husband."

"In that case I will try my hardest to get there." Faith nibbled on the delicious biscuit. "She is an admirable lady." Placing the cup down at her side, she hesitated a moment before taking the small pouch containing the brooch from her pocket. "She gave me a gift for my birthday, and for some reason my Ma was upset and wanted me to return it to her, but I refused." Sucking her bottom lip in, she wondered what had made her admit that. What was it about him that made her want to disclose all her inner secrets to him?

With a surprised glance he reached out, asking, "May I see it?"

Faith nodded as she took it out and passed it to him. "I think it beautiful—and far too extravagant a gift. Perhaps that was the reasoning behind my Ma's stubborn way of thinking. They exchanged words—

most of which I found odd, and the outcome was that Ma told Mrs. Pollock to find other lodgings. Do you sometimes find the ways of the older folk slightly strange? They seem to have a set of rules that they live by that are way beyond what I myself can fathom. Perhaps it is simply that my mother does not want me to consider myself important to others."

Still fingering the brooch, he said, "You could be right there, Faith. My Ma has a saying that she tosses my way when she feels I am behaving in a way she doesn't consider seemly. 'Don't get too big for your boots young man', she says." He grinned as he handed the brooch back. "It certainly is a beautiful gift."

"And far too valuable I fear for me to wear. When am I likely to have a ball gown that would do it justice?" Faith ran a finger over the blue stones. "Mrs. Pollock said that it was valuable, and the day might come when I would find its value useful. What do you think?"

"I think she is a very sensible lady, and no doubt there was some thought behind the gift." He put his cup into the basket and then rested back on his elbows, looking to a fluffy cloud overhead, as he asked, "Do you ever dream of getting away from here, Faith? Perhaps travelling to far distant places in this huge country—to places where only a few white folks have been?"

For a moment, Faith looked into the distance where a man leading his donkey was obviously heading to the crushing battery. "To be honest, I dream of escaping this life I have here, Walt. I know I should feel lucky when compared to others of similar age but being selfish I do want more."

"That's not being selfish, silly woman. That is called an honest dream. This colony was founded on the dreams of men, and oft times of women seeking a better lot in life." He too stared into the distance for a while.

Faith took the opportunity to look closely at his face, a face she found very attractive. A lock of his wayward hair blew across his eyes, and he pushed it back carelessly with a strong hand. Something inside Faith melted and she imagined what life would be like if she ran off with him. "What would your Ma and Papa say if you told them you wished to head elsewhere?" she asked.

Turning to her, a grin split his face before he said, "I never thought that far ahead to be truthful. I had a childhood dream, and it was perhaps breeding and raising horses one day. I keep that close to my chest now as my Pa would not relish losing his best delivery man, and Ma is like most mothers I reckon—would not like to see her youngest son go off to seek greener pastures." His mouth twisted wryly as he added, "My brother George caused a ruckus I can tell you when he decided to move to Melbourne not a month after he wed."

"Do you hear from him, and has he prospered down there?"

"Oh yes, we received a message only last week that he sent on the mail wagon. His time in the store served him well and now he and his bride run an emporium for some wealthy trader that he was lucky to meet."

"And where did your dream of raising horses come from, Walt?" Faith guessed that he had a great affection for his mare, but this declaration surprised her."

With a grin, he said, "When I was a lad one of my Pa's regular customers would sit me down and tell these great yarns of his years working for a man who trained horses that were entered in races. His life sounded like one I would like to lead one day, but it was not to be. When I told my Pa of this dream, he reckoned it was a load of nonsense, and I should stick to following in his footsteps for trading was a safer way to earn a living." A sigh followed this statement.

Faith thought how good it could be to live a life away from the rules and harshness of her Ma. But then guilt struck her—how could she even consider being such an ungrateful daughter. "Perhaps we should be heading back now," she said with a sigh. "Thank you for today, it has been really pleasant." That sounded formal again and she brushed crumbs from her skirt as she made to rise.

Before she moved further, Walt caught her hand and with a slight tug, pulled her back down as he said, "It has been more than pleasant, Faith. It has been the best time of my life, and I have a small favour to ask."

"You do?" she swallowed as she wondered just what he could want of her.

"Perhaps I am swimming up the wrong creek, and you might think I am asking liberties of you, for you think of me as nothing more than a friend, but could I perhaps have a small kiss. 'Tis something I have thought about often since our first meeting."

"It is?" Staring at his mouth, now hovering very close to hers, she nodded, knowing there was nothing in this world that she would take more delight in. Impulsively she touched his lips with a fingertip and heard his deep gulp before his mouth covered hers. Nothing before in her life had brought so much pleasure.

Without knowing how it happened, she was lying on her back and his body was half covering hers. Having no idea if the way she felt was normal when being kissed by a man who had filled her many daydreams, she gave herself up to the magic of the moment, knowing deep down that she would hold this memory dear for the rest of her life, no matter what came after.

Cupping her cheeks in hands slightly roughened by hard work, he pulled back a fraction and whispered, "Forgive me, Faith, darling girl, but I think that I did take liberties with you that I should not have."

"You did? Do you mean that I should not have let you kiss me?" His warm breath fanned her cheeks as he placed light kisses on both before sitting up. "I enjoyed it, so I am sure that I am probably now what my Ma calls a fallen woman." Knowing her cheeks flamed, she sent him a small smile.

His roar of laughter sent a couple of cockatoos flying off in annoyance. "Faith, my darling girl, you are the furthest from a fallen woman that any girl can be. It is one of the things I like so much about you—not that I know a lot about fallen women," he added hurriedly. Stroking her warm cheek, he placed another small kiss on her lips before slowly rising. As he pulled her to her feet, he took her in his arms, and she could feel the full length of his strong body as he bent to kiss her again. "If you decide to run away at any time, please let me accompany you. I will be your willing servant." This was said with a distinct smile in his words. "I can

72

think of no better travelling companion. We will seek our destinies together."

Not quite sure if he was jesting with her, or was sincere, Faith said nothing, watching him as he folded the blanket, and then put it and the basket back into the cart. With a shrill whistle, he brought Bob back at a run—he'd spent his time romping with a dog belonging to one of the miners. With tongue lolling, he grinned happily, his tail wagging fit to drop off. The pair had obviously made it down to the river for he was still damp from his swim.

Only as they were on the way home did Walt ask, "Would you care to do this again, Faith?"

"You mean spend the afternoon with you?" Knowing she would love to spend the rest of her life with him, she felt that perhaps that was a foolish question. If he was willing to repeat this time with her, then it could be he felt the same way. Faith realised that her knowledge of men's feelings was so slight that there could be a chance he was teasing her. If that were the case, then it would surely break her heart.

"Exactly, or as we discussed, if you felt the desire to run away from your life here, I would be very happy to be your travelling companion." Once again, she was unsure if he meant this, as he said it with a chuckle.

"You know that is just a fanciful dream, Walt. I thought we were playing a game of make-believe."

Pulling Matilda to a halt, he looked intently at Faith before saying. "I will never play games with you Faith, you must believe that." He took his hat off and ran a hand through his hair. "I feel deep down that you are not happy with your life as it is. Mrs. Pollock no doubt sensed such and that I believe is why she presented you with your treasure trinket. Let me know if you want it valued at any time and I am willing to take it to a reliable merchant who would offer you the best price."

So involved in his kisses and his charm, Faith had completely forgotten about the brooch. Thrusting a hand into her skirt pocket, she wrapped her fingers around the small sachet. Not knowing how to respond to that she sucked in her bottom lip and thought about his offer. With a flap of the reins, he encouraged Matilda into a walk, and the rest of the journey home was in silence.

With heavy heart, she allowed him to assist her down outside the lodging house. Would he keep his word and repeat this outing, or would this afternoon be all she had to remember for the remainder of her days? About to say something, her thoughts were interrupted by her Ma's shout of, "And just where do you think you have been gallivanting for hours at a time, young woman?"

Walt saved her from replying by doffing his hat and with a small bow, saying, "Faith allowed me to escort her home, Mrs. Boswell, as it looked about to rain when she was ready to set out." That was so obviously a lie for there was not a cloud in the sky.

Her Ma's response to that was to look up, and mutter something unintelligible. Walt sent Faith a wink before heading around the cart and climbing aboard. Expecting her Ma to send further questions her way, Faith scurried up the passage and out to the outhouse at the rear of the garden.

When she returned to the kitchen, Bertha was preparing a pie for the lodger's late meal. "So, how did it go?" she asked with a grin. "Did you enjoy your outing."

"Oh, yes, Bertha. It was the best time of my life." Faith's cheeks were warm as she came around the table and whispered, "Walt kissed me."

"He did, did he? And I am guessing you enjoyed it." Bertha laughed as she lay a hand on Faith's cheek.

Faith nodded as she also grinned. "Am I now considered a bad woman, Bertha? You know, one of those that Ma calls a tart?"

"Goodness gracious me, but you are a soft one, girl. It is only right that when a girl reaches seventeen, she should have shared at least one kiss from a handsome boy."

"He is handsome, isn't he? And he is so kind, Bertha, and he calls his mare Matilda, would you believe?"

"Any man who names his horse such must be considered a real gentleman."

They shared another laugh at that like a pair of conspirators, but then Gert burst into the kitchen, glaring at them before demanding, "What is so funny it is keeping the pair of you from your chores? Time you set the tables, my girl, instead of wasting Bertha's time with your nonsense."

Still so entranced was Faith that even her Ma's stiff tongue could not dull the glow within her as Faith obeyed.

* * *

It was excessively hot for a November day, and Faith fanned her face with a hand as she hurried along the street, hoping that she would see Walt as she passed the store. On her way at last to visit Mrs. Pollock, she cast a furtive look over her shoulder. As luck would have it there had been a small mishap in the pantry and one of the shelves had come loose, spilling its contents onto the dirt floor. The man who

76

did odd jobs that encompassed everything, be it repairing shelves or something trivial that could not be done by Bertha or her Ma, was summoned. So engrossed was Gert in giving him orders that she did not notice Faith slipping out, bonnet in hand.

To her delight, Walt came from the store, the usual grin on his face, a face that had appeared in all of Faith's dreams since their outing. Doffing his hat he asked, "Are you coming in to buy something today, fair Faith?"

"No, I am hoping to catch a few moments at last with Mrs. Pollock. I managed to slip away while my Mama was busy."

"In that case I will not keep you, as I guess you do not have time to dally." About to go back into the store, he turned to ask, "When do you think we will be able to repeat our pleasant outing? That is of course if you are interested in repeating it."

Faith put a hand to her mouth. She had longed for him to ask her since their outing and was beginning to wonder if he had lost interest in her completely. "I would like it very much," she said, hoping she did not sound too eager. "I must hurry off now, so perhaps we could talk when next I bring in the grocery list."

"Of course. Enjoy your meeting with Madam Pollock. I should not have kept you so long." With a small bow he turned and went inside.

Faith's heart felt light as she went on her way. The hotel in Lydiard Street was one of the finest in Ballarat, and as she entered the door, she felt slightly awed. In comparison to their lowly lodging house, it seemed like a great mansion to her. A man came towards her asking, "Can I help you at all young miss?"

"I am here to see Mrs. Pollock. Could you direct me to her room please? She is expecting me." That was not exactly true and for a moment Faith faltered, hoping this was not a wasted journey.

"Ah, now just go down that passage, and you will find the lady in the last room along on the left." Saying that, he turned and went through a door behind a desk.

Faith rapped with a knuckle on the door, now feeling slightly nervous for some reason. Perhaps the dear lady had forgotten her request for a visit. But in no time the door was opened and to Faith's complete surprise Bryce Witherton stood there holding it wide. With a small smile he said, "What a pleasant surprise, my dear. Look who is here," he turned to say to Mrs. Pollock who sat by a small writing desk.

"Well, what a surprise for sure. Come here and sit by me, I was beginning to think you had forgotten this old woman." She gestured to a chair beside her as she flapped at her face with a brightly coloured fan. Faith wondered why no windows were open to let in the small waft of air that might have cooled the stifling room.

"Oh no, far from it, Madam, I just have not been able to get away." After removing her bonnet and placing it on a side table, Faith sat primly, hands folded in her lap.

Mrs. Pollock's mouth twisted in a small grimace. "I understand dear. How is that mother of yours these days?" There was not a hint of true interest in the question.

"The same. I cannot stay long as she will wonder why I was out. More importantly, how is your health? Are you well attended to by the staff here?"

A small chuckle escaped the lady's mouth as she tapped the fan on Faith's knee. "No one will every care for me as you did, my dear." Drawing in a deep breath she then said, "That is why I have a small proposition to put to you, Faith."

Faith's head went back. What on earth could this person who barely knew her have to offer her? "You have?" She stared at Mrs. Pollock as she waited for what could be coming next.

Before she could say another word, Bryce Witherton patted the old lady on the shoulder, saying, "I will leave you lovely ladies to your discussion." Bowing in front of them both, he then strode to the door and departed.

Mrs. Pollock pulled at the sleeves of her dull coloured muslin gown and drew in a deep breath. "Fact of it is dear Faith, my health is deteriorating and according to the doctor it is all due to my ageing bones." She sighed and leant forward to tap Faith on the knee. "Happens to us all, according to this doctor fellow. Not a lot we can do to hold back the sands of time." Settling back, she stared for a while towards the window.

Impatient to hear about this suggested proposition Faith said, "I am sorry you have to endure pain; it must make life difficult."

"Very—but as I think I told you—or maybe not, I am thinking of going back to Melbourne. Mr. Witherton, kind gentleman that he is, has offered me a room in his house in exchange for certain small tasks that I could do without exerting myself too much."

"That is very thoughtful of him." Faith had no idea what else to add to that. There was obviously some link between the two of them for him to make such an offer. Good manners decreed she say no more.

"I suppose you are wondering why he should make such a suggestion. As you might well have guessed we did not meet casually here in this town. The big house I worked in where I told you my late husband also worked was owned by Mr. Witherton's parents."

Fact was, Faith had come to that conclusion. Without saying anything, she nodded.

"It seems that his journey here with its reasons for such has been a somewhat fruitless exercise—almost. One thing of value has come from it." With a small cough and a wave of the hand she added, "More of that later. Now I will get back to the proposition mentioned earlier." Peering intently at Faith she continued, "I feel you are not wholly happy with your lot in life my dear. Through no fault of your own, it seems that your mother resents your presence. I would like to remedy that and ask if you would accompany me to Mr. Witherton's residence in Melbourne where you could be of assistance to me—act as a sort of maid." Her eyes held a question as she peered at Faith.

With a hand to her chest, Faith stared back at her in astonishment. Deep down she had to admit that she had half expected such as soon as the lady mentioned it. Momentarily the idea of fleeing with this kind lady seemed a wondrous idea. To start a new life far away from the day-to-day drudgery imposed on her sounded like a fairy tale. But then reality struck her. As difficult as life was, Gertrude was still her mother and deserved some respect, if she was to be honest with herself.

And then another thought crept in—would she not rather run away to a new life with Walt as he had suggested? How would he react if she told him she was going to Melbourne town with this lady? Weighing both options, she knew which by far she would prefer. "But I cannot just leave my Mama who has never mistreated me and has provided me with a better life than some are forced to live. What would I tell her?"

"You can tell her that you have been offered a life free of being treated like a chattel, my dear. You would live comfortably in a big house with servants to do the fetching and carrying. All I would expect of you is assistance with dressing and bathing and as my problems worsen perhaps in other day to day tasks."

"And when would you be expecting to leave and return to Melbourne?"

"Mr. Witherton is determined to leave while the weather is fine. Although the road has improved since the miners first began to head this way, it is still not suitable to travel when it is likely to be wet."

"And would you expect me to leave without giving my Ma warning or excuse? I fear I could never do such a thing to her regardless of how I have longed to live another life."

"That is your problem, Faith my girl, you have a kind heart. Lord above knows how you have kept your loving and thoughtful nature in the face of such adversity." Rising, she reached for a walking cane and slowly hobbled over to a small chest standing at the side of the room. Opening a drawer, she pulled out a small wallet and took something from it. After looking at the contents for a moment, she came back and handed a small card to Faith. Pointing to the drawing of a large and handsome house that was depicted on it, she said, "Would it not be every young girls' dream to live in such a place?"

"I admit that it looks splendid, but I am still confused, and although I can understand why he is allowing you to stay there, I am confused as to why Mr. Witherton would allow me to share such a mansion."

"You are by no means an ignorant servant girl, Faith, even if your Mama treats you as such, and I am certain that you have worked it out by now, even if you have not totally admitted it to yourself. The good man is of course your father. Why do you think that your mother was so reluctant to let him into your lives?"

Chapter Five

Faith stumbled as she began to hasten her steps. No doubt her Ma would be in a foul temper wondering where she was and why she had been gone for so long? Mrs. Pollock was not wrong, of course. The realisation that her Ma had lied all Faith's life about her parentage had been in her head since Bryce Witherton's unusual visits, but to hear it so bluntly stated had stunned her.

Such was her state of confusion that she did not see Walt until he stood in front of her on the street. "Oh," she muttered. "I did not see you."

"Obviously. Is something wrong, Faith? You were almost running blindly." Concern filled his words. Bob appeared and sat before Faith looking up at her. Even the dog seemed to sense that something was amiss.

"I…I had a shock. I must get home now as my Ma will be angry, for I have been away too long." Faith glanced about as if her Ma was about to jump out at her. "I need to talk. Do you think we could meet, perhaps tomorrow? I have a decision to make."

"That sounds very mysterious. Of course we can meet." Walt waved to a passing wagon driver who called out to him.

"I must go now. I am so late already. Could I come to the store about the middle of the day at some time?" Without waiting for his response, she hastened on. Bob followed her for a few paces until Walt's whistle sent him back.

Her Ma stood in the passageway as soon as Faith closed the door behind her. "Just where have you been, do you realise we had no idea where you were or what you were up to?" Shaking a fist towards Faith she was almost snarling the words. In that moment Faith felt something akin to hatred for this woman who had given birth to her but for certain held not an ounce of affection for her.

"Bertha knew where I was and I am not a prisoner in this house, Mama. I chose to visit someone and did nothing wrong." Faith straightened her shoulders and defiantly outstared her Ma.

"Did nothing wrong?" This came out at almost a shriek and there was no doubt that her Ma's limbs shook with her anger. "Did you know where she was?" she turned to demand of Bertha who had come out of the kitchen to stand behind her. Bertha shrugged but said nothing before turning and going back to her kitchen. "Visit who?" Gert demanded.

"A friend." All fear had fled, and Faith was engulfed then in a new sense of courage as she said, "I do have friends Mama, believe it or not, and I have every right to pay them a call. That is of course, unless I am indeed a prisoner in this house."

"Every right? Every right?" It appeared that she was so angry all sensible thought had deserted her Ma, who now turned and went into their bedroom, slamming the door so hard Faith feared it would fall into the passageway.

Going into the kitchen Faith sat at the table and put her head in her hands. Bertha set a hand on her shoulder, asking, "How did your visit go, my dear?" She then sat beside her.

Faith swiped at her cheeks where a couple of tears had escaped. "Why is my Ma so awful Bertha? Is it such a crime to visit people or to go out and do things other than be here and beholden to her all the time?"

"Oh, Faith my girl, of course you have every right to a life worth living. I think your Ma is perhaps finding it difficult to understand that you are not a child any longer." She patted Faith's hand again. "Now tell me, how is the old lady Pollock faring and what did she have to say?"

"I can hardly believe it, Bertha, but she wants me to go to Melbourne with her to assist her as she becomes frailer. But more astonishing is that we would be living in Bryce Witherton's house." Faith rubbed at her cheeks again. "It seems that man is my real father and that would account for my Ma's odd behaviour when he came calling."

"I think you half guessed that did you not?" Bertha grinned. "He's a fine figure of a man, anyone would have to say, don't you think?"

Faith nodded. "I still have to find out lots more, and I think my mother would be most unlikely to disclose the true facts. If she cannot face the truth of it, then I suppose I can never persuade her to tell me everything. It now becomes clear that his Mama did not approve of my Ma and therefore tossed her out of the house when they learnt that she was with child." Faith heaved a sigh. "Why could my Ma not tell me the truth? Why tell so many lies? If the gent had not arrived at our door as he did, none of this would have ever come to light."

"Truth has a way of coming out in strange ways, Faith dear."

"I can understand why Mama hated Mr. Witherton's mother—and likely his Papa too, but she must have cared for the man who fathered me. I am not wholly sure of what occurs between two people who share their affection enough to make a baby."

87

"That is another poor example of your Mama's lack of fairness. Such facts should have been disclosed to you quite a few years ago. She had no right to keep you in ignorance of such things." Bertha rubbed at her forehead. "Of course, there could be another reasonable explanation for the whole mess." Placing an arm about Faith's shoulders she said low, "I think it is probably unlikely, but he could have forced himself on your Ma and that would account for her disgust and refusal to have anything to do with him."

"But...but, he is a gentleman, and surely would not commit such a sin. I thought such behaviour was only carried out by the lower class and less educated."

Bertha sighed. "Sadly dearie, it is unfortunately the case that many such gentlemen take advantage of the below stairs staff. Many a kitchen maid or a lowly member of a household finds herself in the same predicament as your Ma obviously did. And it is usual that they are unceremoniously thrown out of the premises without any means of proving their innocence."

"I suppose my Mama was fortunate that the man I thought was my father took care of her and provided a home for her." A sudden thought came into her head and Faith added, "Do you think perhaps that that they were never wed in a church before

God? Once I recall I did ask Mama to tell me about her wedding day and the dress she wore. I must have seen a picture in a newspaper of a great wedding that had taken place in Melbourne and thought the bride looked wonderful in her gown. Ma of course shook her head and told me that not everyone could afford such splendid finery, and I should stop asking foolish questions."

Bertha pushed herself up and blew out a big breath. "It's a fact of course that many do not say their vows before a priest, especially folk of the lower classes. For one reason or another mayhap your Ma and this other man never did get wed. There's a good chance you will never learn the truth of it, Faith. If your Ma has kept such secrets to herself for all this time, she is most likely not about to start changing now. I must get on or I will hear a tongue lashing from her."

"I am so glad I can talk to you, Bertha." Faith put her arms about Bertha's shoulders.

Gert chose that moment to come back into the kitchen. "Isn't it about time the pair of you thought of serving dinner? The men are getting impatient." Her glare should have had Faith shaking in her shoes, but she chose to ignore the reprimand and the night continued without mishap or further scolding.

Much to Faith's surprise, not another word was said on her absence or reason for visiting Mrs. Pollock in the next two days. Faith went about the daily chores, as the good lady's suggestion rolled around in her brain, desperate to find a way to talk it over with Walt. If her Ma had been so angry at her being out for a few hours, what would her reaction be if Faith disclosed that she was thinking of leaving her house and going to Melbourne? Following on that thought, came another—if she decided to accept the offer would it be best if she just left in the night, never to return? That thought brought other fears along with it. Never had she been away from her Ma or made decisions of her own. Perhaps it was time for her to sally forth into a world she never thought to inhabit.

The time came when escape was possible. Clutching the shopping list in her hand, she headed for the store, praying inwardly that Walt would be there and not so busy that he could not spare time to talk with her for a while. As luck would have it his Ma was alone in the store, which thankfully was quiet, except for two old men sorting through various shovels and tools near the back. "Is Walt about?" Faith asked tentatively as she handed her list to Daisy Finch.

"I believe he is out in the yard tending to his horse, Faith. Go along through the door yonder. I'm certain he can spare you the time of day." With a wave of the hand, she gestured to the door in the shadows. Once again Faith was struck by the difference between her and her own Ma. How could two women be so far apart in their approach to life?

"Thank you." As she went past them, the two gents who were haggling now gave her a look of indifference before continuing their argument.

The yard behind the store was much larger that their one at home. Going past the stack of crates and boxes beside a huge shed, she heard Walt's voice as he crooned softly. Bob must have heard her approach for he bounded towards her and licked her hand as she greeted him. Together they went through the door. Walt was in the process of working on one of Matilda's hooves. He was stripped to the waist and in the moment before he looked up and saw Faith, she admired his strong body. Seldom had she seen a half naked man except for the natives who chose to go around part clothed. In fact, the only time was when one of the miners ran through town waving his discarded shirt in his glee at finding a nugget of gold.

"You have a nice voice," she said, knowing her voice came out huskily. With a small cough she quickly added, "I hope I have not caught you when you are very busy."

Reaching for his shirt which he pulled on slowly, he laughed. "Never too busy for you, Faith. I am about ready for a rest." Stroking the mare's neck, he told her to continue with whatever was in her manger, and beckoned Faith to a bench. "Come sit here. No one will bother us, and it is cooler here inside. It is warming up as we near Yuletide."

Feeling ridiculously shy, she sat and straightened her skirt over her knees. "As I told you, I have a decision to make, and I hoped you could help me to sort out my jumbled thoughts."

"I will do my best—but I am just a simple bloke so don't expect me to solve any difficult dilemmas you might have." This was followed by a chuckle.

Faith felt deep down that he was no simple fellow at all. "I went to visit with Mrs. Pollock as you know, and she shocked me to my bones by saying she wishes me to accompany her back to Melbourne to be some sort of companion. She more or less needs assistance with her failing health as she grows older."

Rubbing at his head where his hair was already dishevelled, he asked, "And when does she intend to return to Melbourne town?" Faith could not be certain but sensed he was not pleased with her news.

"Well, fact is that she will be living in the home of Mr. Witherton, and so will be travelling back with him. He wishes to go while the weather is still favourable as the road begins to be troublesome in the winter months." Faith nibbled on the end of her thumb. Walt seemed surprised—or stunned at her news.

"So, this means that you will also be living in this gent's house I take it?" Rising, he went to Matilda's side and stood stroking her neck. Bob sat looking up at Faith as if he waited on whatever was coming next.

"Yes. They seem to share some bond. I do know that she went to work in his parent's home about the time that my Ma left."

"This all seems to be odd; do you not think?" He sat beside her again and stared at his boots.

"How so?"

"Let's see. The lady takes a room in your Ma's house—apparently after her husband was killed. He brought her to the diggings in the hope of finding gold, or so she claimed. But then this gent comes along from your Ma's past claiming you are his daughter. Your Ma refuses—for reasons she will not disclose—to have anything to do with him." He stroked at a palm as he shook his head. "Sounds fishy to me, Faith. Then, after your Ma tosses her out of your lodging house she ends up at the same fine hotel as this gent. Now, if she worked for him years ago, don't it seem odd to you that the pair of them meet up again so many years later and hatch this plan to get you in his home on the assumption you will be her skivvy or similar?"

Lost for words, she fiddled with the strings of her bonnet on her lap. Of course, all this or similar had gone through her head in the nights she had gone over and over the events of the past few weeks. Did Walt consider her a foolish girl for even considering this offer? "You are telling me that I am stupid for even thinking of leaving. Do you recall we talked about getting away from here? I thought this would be a good way to do it. There would be employment for me, a nice house to live in. Mrs. Pollock is obviously fond of me, as the gentleman is it seems. What does my future hold if I stay here, Walt? With a Ma who does not care one whit for me, and an uncertain future."

"When I spoke of getting away, I meant the two of us, Faith. What about me, is there not one thought in your head about leaving me? I thought that you at least cared for me in some small way." He jumped up and strode away to stand by the door, a hand to the back of his head.

Faith went to stand by him, placing a hand on his arm. "You could come with me. I would have asked you that had you thought my leaving was a good idea. When you think about it, you may be able to work for Mr. Witherton. Or perhaps you could join your brother who you said is doing well down south."

Shaking his head, he stared down at her before taking her cheeks in his palms. "I had this dream of the two of us running away and free, not of me working for a man who when all is said and done is your father. Who knows how your life will change once you are under his care? Once in his house he will have complete control over you. Do you even have any inkling of what sort of person he is? The world out there is so different to the sheltered one that you know, Faith. As I see it, you may end up with fine clothes and all the trappings of the upper class, but for all you know you could be trapped in a life not to your liking—and it will be harder to escape from that one once accepted."

Suddenly remembering the time and realising that she had been away longer than expected she said, "I must go now, Walt. My Ma will be wondering why I have been gone so long."

"I am sorry that I have done little to help you with your decision, Faith. All I ask is that you think it through very carefully. Visit the lady again and ask her for more details. If you are indeed Mr. Witherton's daughter, then he might wish to treat you as such and not expect you to fetch and carry for her."

As she sped home, Walt's words of wisdom raced around in her brain. He was so right—everything now had taken on a new meaning and needed careful thought. She thought of the brooch, probably the crux of all this. It now seemed likely the gift had come from him, for if it was so valuable how could her husband, a mere stable man, have ever afforded such a trinket. Far from assisting her with her problem, Walt had made matters a deal worse by putting all these other obstacles in the way.

As she expected, her Ma looked cross and flustered when Faith entered the kitchen. "How long does a simple errand take you, my girl. Have you been dallying with that Walter Finch again?"

"I did talk to him, he is a nice young man, Ma. I cannot see anything wrong in spending a few moments in his company." Faith threw her bonnet onto the dresser.

"Anything wrong?" This came out as a near screech, and Bertha signalled with her eyes and a shake of the head that to argue with her would be pointless.

"What shall I do?" Faith decided it best to ignore the outburst.

Later, after the dinner dishes were all put away, and Faith and Bertha were alone in the kitchen, she asked, "Did the young fellow have any words of wisdom to offer you?"

Faith shrugged. "I fear he has only put more disturbing thoughts into my head. I guess there is truth in his suspicion that once under Bryce Witherton's roof, he might consider he would have full control over me as his dependant. Oh, Bertha, I am so confused." Sitting at the table, Faith put her face in her palms.

"It's a big decision to make, my dear girl. Take your time thinking it over."

Wise words, but Faith already had an aching head for fretting over it. Once the decision was made and they were on the way to Melbourne there would be no turning back.

* * *

As Christmas neared, the weather took a turn for the worse and it rained heavily for a few days which made the air more humid. On her way to the store Faith dodged the puddles, her head down as she pulled the hood of her cloak over her head. Since the day when she had discussed her problem with Walt, she had only seen him when he delivered their order. Hoping it was her imagination, she fretted that he had lost interest in her. He seemed as friendly as ever but said nought about her decision which only made her more certain that he was not worried one way or the other anymore.

Her Ma had never made much of a celebration at Christmastide, so Faith had got used to receiving no gifts from her, but nonetheless she always made some small present for Bertha. This year it was a neckerchief that she had embroidered around the edges. Bertha liked to wear something around her neck when the heat in the kitchen made her perspire.

A carriage pulled up beside her, and Faith ignored it until a call from Mrs. Pollock alerted her. "How are you my dear," the older lady asked as she beckoned Faith nearer. When Faith stood beside the window she added, "I expected a visit from you before now. Did you consider my offer of employment? I must tell you that Mr. Witherton is eager to begin the journey to his home and would have left but for the heavy rain which would likely make the road very unmanageable in parts."

Faith was still digesting the fact that the woman was travelling in his coach like a member of the gentry. Was there a touch of a reprimand in her tone? Befuddled, she shook her head, uncertain what to say. "I have not been able to make up my mind, Madam, and we have been extraordinarily busy at the house with new lodgers arriving."

"And I take it that mother of yours has been hounding you off your feet." She opened the door. "Come inside for a moment, Faith, out of the rain."

Faith hesitated but then mounted the step and sat opposite Mrs. Pollock. "I cannot stay long as I have this list to deliver to the store." She waved it in front of her.

With a sigh the lady shook her head. "Tut, it seems your Ma is still working you like a slave. Now if you accept my offer, not only will you be expected to work less, but you will be doing it in much more agreeable conditions than you currently toil in." Touching her wrinkled forehead, she glanced out of the window, before adding, "I suggest that you give it serious thought, young woman, for such a chance might never come again."

"I will, I promise." Faith put her hand on the door catch in preparation of climbing down, and Mrs. Pollock placed her gloved one over it, staying her.

"Think on this, my dear. I was a simple downstairs maid, treated with little kindness by my employers when I was your age. Until I met my dear departed husband, I had only known hard work and poor conditions. But now dear Mr. Witherton has seen fit to treat me as an equal and offered me a place in his grand home—not below stairs with the servants but with an apartment of my own. His desire is to offer you a better life than you have so far experienced, and as his own flesh and blood you would never want for anything."

Faith nodded and climbed down. Turning back as the door closed, she promised, "I will give you my answer within a day or two."

"You do that, dear child, and think well on my words." With that she banged her stick on the roof of the carriage and Faith stood there watching it as it trundled off.

Walt was at the door of the store when Faith reached it. "I see you were talking to Mrs. Pollock," he said, as Faith bent to stroke Bob. "Does that mean that your decision is made?"

Chewing on her lip, she shook her head. "No, Walt, it does not. She was simply telling me of the opportunity that lay ahead of me and pointing out the benefits, which are many."

"With benefits come drawbacks. I have come to a decision myself. Should you choose to go, I will perhaps follow you—just to ensure that you are safe and happy in your new life."

"You have?" Faith gaped at him. "Have you told your Ma and Pa?"

"I did mention to them that I would like to take a trip down south—on the excuse that I would like to visit George and his wife who are expecting a child in the New Year. They were none too pleased but know they can easily find a replacement man to take on the deliveries in my absence."

Faith doubted that, for he was a harder worker than most, but was not about to say so, for she knew deep down that she had been waiting on hearing this from him. After spending many a disturbed night of worrying, it was the thought of never seeing Walt again that had mostly been holding her back. "I am still not sure if I should tell my Ma, or if I should just leave without a word." The thought of her Ma's anger was enough to make her consider slipping away one day without warning.

Walt shrugged. "Only you know best about that."

* * *

As expected, Christmas Day went by without incident. It was a day like most others in their household with them feeding the men on their return each evening. As was the way in the town, their lodgers changed continually as new prospective miners arrived and then left after staking a claim or moving on elsewhere. Some were just wanderers in search of gaining a spot with a set-up miner. Most could not afford to stay in lodgings more than one or two nights but enjoyed a cooked meal and a chance to scrub off the grime of the road. Her Ma had considered—temporarily—to offer some sort of bathing, but then abandoned the idea for it would entail drawing and heating water and then emptying the tub, tasks that she would need to pay someone to carry out. She considered that most could be satisfied with a dip in the river anyway.

The rain eased and the ground soon began to harden in the heat that became sweltering. After paying a hasty visit to Mrs. Pollock she now knew that if she wished to travel with them, it would be soon after the start of the new year, 1861.

"It's my belief that you would be wise not to tell your Ma of your decision," Bertha advised after Faith relayed her news. "Knowing the rage she can get herself into, I have a feeling she would do something drastic to prevent your going."

"I will miss you so, Bertha. How will I manage without your wisdom?"

"You will manage well enough, young lady. It is well past time for you to go out into the world yonder and discover the new life that has been offered you by the grace of God." More to do with the grace of Mr. Witherton, Faith thought, but said naught.

Much as it went against Faith's nature to be so secretive, in the deep of a sleepless night she made the decision to slip out early on the morning of their departure. That way hopefully her Ma would not become suspicious and come hastily searching for her.

Bertha arranged to fabricate excuses for her absence thus they would be well on their way to Melbourne before she realised Faith was not coming back. Mrs. Pollock had already advised it best to travel light and therefore she would not need to pack a bag. "Mr. Witherton has already stressed to me that he is prepared to supply you with all the necessary requirements of a young lady. Therefore, you just need what you travel in."

As the day drew near, panic set in and Faith began to shake for no reason. "What in heaven's name is wrong with you girl?" her Ma complained when Faith almost dropped a pile of dishes she was carrying to the kitchen. Flustered, Faith mumbled an excuse of a headache, something she never suffered from, which made her Ma suspicious. "Best take a dose of those Holloway pills that are supposed to cure most illnesses."

"I think it is just my monthly bleeding, Ma, that plus the heat." That was no lie, for her Ma had seen her rummaging around for rags only last evening. Thankful it had worked out so, Faith was glad that would not be another problem to cope with on the day of travel.

So it was that on the fourth day of the New Year, Faith said a tearful goodbye to Bertha, who ensured that Faith had the brooch safely tucked into the pocket of her skirt and crept from the house. She carried a small purse containing the few other personal articles she was taking, such as her brush and comb and a ribbon or two for her braid. The sun began to peep over the horizon as she moved swiftly along the street. A few men shuffled past on their way about their business and ignored her. Faith's insides were in turmoil and momentarily she considered turning back.

Chapter Six

"Now you make yourselves comfortable, ladies, and we will be on our way shortly," the man Faith had been told was their driver Chapman, said as he closed the door of the carriage. Doubting she would be able to settle comfortably at all, Faith sat back, her fingers fidgeting in her lap.

Mrs. Pollock patted her hands and said comfortingly, "No doubt you are on tenterhooks dear, but do try to relax. Mr. Witherton was overjoyed that you decided to come along."

That did little to allay her nervousness. Not once had he passed many words with her after the day when she visited Mrs. Pollock in the hotel, and Faith was beginning to wonder if he was at all interested in her or could simply be allowing Mrs. Pollock the comfort of having assistance as she got frailer.

"Are you certain of this?" Faith asked as she caught sight of the gentleman in question as he passed a few words with his driver Chapman, a man she estimated to not be a lot older than his master.

"Most certain my dear. He is as excited as a boy, you will see."

Doubting that, Faith peered out of the window anxiously. Where was Walt? At their last meeting he said he would be riding his mare Matilda and would follow on behind the coach. When she asked after Bob, he assured her that his faithful dog would be joining him, saying that he was quite capable of keeping pace. Faith had been puzzled as to why he did not seek employment with the man who was her father and Walt said that he far preferred making his own way. She had a feeling that he somehow did not wholly trust Bryce Witherton while wondering what he based this mistrust on.

To her surprise the carriage began to move off, and he did not come to sit along with them. "I think your father has decided to sit up front alongside Chapman," Mrs. Pollock said. "No doubt he did not wish to spend long hours with a pair of chattering females." This was said with a small laugh.

Faith leaned over and took another look out of the window as they trundled towards the edges of town but still Walt was nowhere in sight. Another carriage was a short way behind them and a smaller wagon behind that. Faith presumed folk preferred to travel in a group for safety. Because she was still a child when they first came to Ballarat, she could not recall a lot about the journey up from Melbourne only that it seemed to take forever. Most of all she remembered feeling sick as the coach bumped across endless ruts and creeks. Walt told her that depending on the strength of Witherton's horses they would probably be rested about halfway to Melbourne.

"Now is the time to say so if you have any regrets, Faith dear," the old lady said as they neared the end of the main street and houses became sparser. She seemed to sense Faith's anxiety, not knowing that it was mostly due to Walt's absence.

Faith shook her head, while thinking that she could descend from the coach now and still make it home before her Ma got too suspicious. "No, I have made my decision," she said, taking one final glance from the window. The vehicles behind them were throwing up a dust cloud, which made it difficult to see past them anyway. There was still time for Walt to catch up with them when they stopped to rest the horses. Perhaps he decided to keep his distance and follow a fair distance behind.

That thought sustained her as they drew further and further away from town and Mrs. Pollock gave her other worries to occupy these thoughts as she said, "I do hope the road is safer than it was when I travelled up with my husband. We heard horrific tales of what the bushrangers did to poor unsuspecting souls travelling north in the old days. Most miners came up on foot, and the road was barely passable in places with the endless carts and wagons. The creeks and streams could be deadly with no such thing as bridges or safe crossings." She rambled on for a while as the movement of the coach made Faith sleepy. Guessing that her lack of sleep over the past week as she prepared for this escape was the reason for her tiredness, she let sleep claim her.

Waking with a start, Faith realised that the coach was stationary. Mrs. Pollock snored and snuffled softly, so as quietly as she could Faith opened the door and stepped down onto hard ground. "Ah, if you wish to relieve yourself missy," Chapman said, "I suggest you use yon stand of trees. But watch for snakes."

That last warning was unnecessary as her Ma had taught her well since a child to steer clear of places where those creatures might hide. "Thank you, Mr. Chapman," she said as she made for the suggested place.

"No need for the mister," he called from behind her. "Just Chapman or Chappie will do. I'll see if your companion wishes to avail herself of the opportunity." This he said with a laugh, and Faith decided she liked him.

Finishing what needed to be done she made her way back towards the coach just as Mrs. Pollock was being helped down by

Chappie. "Come with me, Faith dear," she called. "I need assistance."

While waiting for her to attend to the job at hand, Faith peered along the road in the hope of catching sight of Walt or even Bob, but apart from the other two vehicles whose occupants were also scattered behind various shrubs and gum trees there was no other traveller in sight on the road. Faith put a hand above her eyes to shield them from the sun and estimated it to be not quite noon.

"We will travel for another hour or so and then stop for lunch," Chappie said as he helped them both back into the coach where the heat was becoming oppressive.

"Please ensure you seek out a shaded area," Mrs. Pollock said as she fanned her face, which had turned quite red.

"That I will do, madam, you can be sure," he said with a wink Faith's way.

The man who was her father said little apart from enquiring if they were both comfortable, before they set off again. "Is he always so quiet?" Faith asked.

"I have found that he is one of those people who only speaks when there is something of merit to say. You will perhaps find it unusual. Having been married to a man who could talk the hind leg off a donkey and most of what he said being rubbish, I find it refreshing."

"I was hoping to get to know him better on the journey."

"I fear his mother was a rather overpowering woman and so from a young age Bryce found it best to keep his thoughts to himself."

"You said that you joined the household about the time that my mother was ordered from the house. Do you recall the circumstances that brought about her dismissal? My Ma refused to say one word on the subject, so I have no idea how it came about that he fathered me."

"Ah, I guess you are very curious to know the ins and outs of it all. Sadly, there is little I can add to what you know already. Fact is, I was kept busy running around for the housekeeper, a woman who had little care for the overworked staff in that household—she only cared for feathering her own nest. I do know that Bryce Witherton was a broken man—or boy, I should say. Half the problem was that he and your Mama were barely adults, and his father was no better than his mother, both ensuring Bryce abided by their strict rules."

"What of his Papa? Did he also die, or do they still share a house?" Faith bit her lip. Until now she had not considered that her newly found father might be beneath his Papa's rule still.

Mrs. Pollock patted her knee as she shook her head. "You do not need to worry your head about that one, my dear. The pair are estranged and have been since Bryce's mother died. The old man was furious when his wife's father passed away shortly after her demise and left his grandson a substantial legacy. It is the house he bequeathed to Bryce where we will reside."

Faith mulled that over for a while and then asked, "So how is it that you and Mr. Witherton seem so close?"

She received no answer and when she looked at the older woman's face, her eyes were closed, which left her wondering if the older lady was feigning sleep to dodge answering that question. Left to watch the passing scenery, Faith wondered anew just what awaited her at the end of this journey. Knowing she should be slightly scared, if not terrified, she nonetheless felt a sense of freedom never known before. Just the thought of not being at her Ma's beck and call was enough to lift her spirits. If only Walt had consented to accompany them on the journey, then she might even feel lighthearted.

As Chappie promised, they soon stopped for a break, which true to his word was near a stand of trees and a small creek where the horses could get a drink. Once on their way again Mrs. Pollock was soon asleep, leaving Faith to her thoughts. While lunching on slices of beef and bread her father had asked how they fared but said little else. Faith wondered if she would ever get to know the man well enough to question him on the truth of it all.

To her distress Walt had not appeared as she had hoped. Catching her looking along the road they had travelled, Mrs. Pollock had queried, "Expecting your young man to be coming after us, are you?"

Faith decided not to take that any further and just said a hasty no, but now had plenty of time to go through several emotions, the main one being annoyance. If he had not one notion of following her, then why had he made a promise to do so. But then when Faith thought more on it, she could not quite recall if he had actually promised or just said maybe. Perhaps he was doing what most men did and that was pretending he cared enough to chase after her.

But what did she know of men and their behaviour? Most of the men who stayed in the lodging house were there for such a short time that she barely knew their names let alone what their thoughts were. Most of them only had one subject in mind to discuss between themselves, and that was finding enough gold to become rich. When she thought back on it, the man she had always thought was her father had seemed rather brash with her Ma. As far as Faith knew he was not unkind though, and never raised his hand in anger—not in front of her anyway.

Perhaps Walt was not pleased that rather than run away with him she had decided to come along with Mrs. Pollock and Bryce Witherton to an uncertain future. The niggling annoyance turned to anger as the afternoon wore on. But common sense had to intervene, for it could be that something had happened at home to prevent him coming along. She had ensured that he knew the address where they were headed, so if that were the case all she could hope was that she would receive a letter of explanation.

When Chappie helped them down outside the inn where they were to spend the night, Faith was quite aching all over from the jolting and was not surprised when Mrs. Pollock said she would retire as soon as they had eaten. Once settled in the tiny room they were to share, Faith decided to go outside to stretch her legs as it had cooled somewhat once darkness began to fall.

"Aching a bit is she, the old lady?" Chappie asked, when Faith joined him by a fenced off yard where the horses were nibbling on a patch of grass. He waved the hand holding a pipe towards the road they had just travelled, and said on a laugh, "Not the best travelling along that way, is it?

Though it has much improved of late let me tell you."

"Have you been Mr. Witherton's driver for many years?" she asked, feeling that he would not object to her question, for he seemed to like a chat.

"Well, I began as stable boy when I was still knee high to a grasshopper, and the head stableman assured me I was good at handling the horses so as soon as the position as driver became available, I asked if I could learn. I was already the best at putting on the harness, so I was told." Obviously proud of his achievements he patted himself on the chest as he grinned. One of their bays came to the fence and Chappie stroked its nose as he pulled a bent carrot from his pocket that the horse took very carefully.

"So, you know my father well?" she dared to ask, gratified that he seemed ready to talk.

"Known him since he was little more than a lad like meself," he said with a chuckle. "Went along with him when he set out on his own after the falling out with his Pa." Rubbing at his head he continued, "What a to do that was, but the young fella came off trumps didn't he, thanks to his Ma's father, a curmudgeon of a character, but thank the good Lord, one who did right by the boy."

"So, in that case, you would have been around when the trouble brewed about my Ma and your master, would you not?"

"That I was, young miss, but being a foolish young un meself, I was too busy flirting with the prettiest scullery maid to pay much heed to what went on." A hearty laugh followed that confession.

"My Ma worked in the kitchens or so I thought, so perhaps you knew her, did you?"

"Oh yes, and knew her and the master had a fancy for each other, but then she was made to leave suddenly." Looking into the distance for a bit he then said, "He was like a broken man for some time after she took off, but that harridan of a Ma of his, well she had a mouth on her like a gutter snipe and so he learnt to keep things to himself he did. She made him wed that high and mighty Spanish Zelda woman."

Faith stared at him in shock and blurted, "He is married?"

Chappie shook his head. "Was, but that one died giving birth, didn't she?"

Why hadn't Mrs. Pollock ever told her this? "She had a child? And is this child living with Mr. Witherton?" Faith could not get her head around this new information. Why was she not told this important piece of news? Why had Mrs. Pollock seen fit to omit such a thing? But then Faith chastised herself. Was it really of any importance to her?

"Oh, yes, he's a wag is that young 'un, prefers going out to watch the creatures than learning his lessons, does master James." With a laugh that sent a couple of nesting parrots into a flurry of feathers he pointed the pipe Faith's way and added, "The master lets him run wild, says being young is not the time for stuffy old lessons, but a time for having fun."

That news pleased Faith, proving her new Papa was indeed a kind-hearted man. "Could that be because his own childhood was so disciplined by his mother—who as you said was a harridan with harsh tongue?" Not so different to her own Ma so it seemed.

"Yes, miss, you have hit the old nail on the head there I reckon." He sighed, bashed his pipe on the fence rail and with a small salute said, "Time to hit the sack, miss. We still have a long drive tomorrow."

As he strolled off, Faith stared at the horses, some of which were now lying down, and pondered on the new discovery. A half brother sounded nice. She had always wished for a sister, but a brother would do as well. With a yawn she too went inside. Mrs. Pollock's snores, along with the everything she had learned this night, kept her from sleep for some time.

* * *

"Not far to go now," Mrs. Pollock said as more houses appeared. The road had grown busier in the past hour or so as a few wagons being pulled by hefty bullocks passed them on the road. Carrying goods and belongings of those settling inland, Mrs. Pollock had told Faith. "I suppose you are curious and perhaps a little apprehensive as to what your new life will hold for you are you not?"

Strangely, it was excitement more than anything else that overrode all her apprehensions now. "I am looking forward to meeting my step-brother," Faith said. After hearing about the boy from Chappie she had passed on the discovery to the old lady and asked her why she thought this information had not been disclosed to her before.

"Ah yes, the lad is a strange one I can tell you. I am sure you will like him though. I feel you are not one to make rash judgements." She fanned her face with the elaborately decorated fan she carried with her all the time. "By the way, as we know each other far better, I feel you can call me Polly from now on. After all, I am not mistress of the house and most certainly am not regarded as a lady of importance by Mr. Witherton's staff who all call me by that name."

Faith mulled that over. She was interested to see how the staff acted with this woman who, in fact, was originally a servant in her father's home. Yet to learn exactly why she was to be given a room of her own in the house, Faith looked forward to learning a lot more truth about many things once she was settled.

As more and more houses appeared at each side of the road, there seemed to be a lot of activity with wagons, carriages and farm carts now going in both directions, causing quite a dust up as the heat became oppressive and Mrs. Pollock's fan worked hard.

Dusk was falling as the carriage came to a halt and Polly said with a heartfelt sigh, "We have arrived."

Faith had been looking with keen interest at the passing houses, some with well tended gardens at their fronts, and some half hidden behind tall gates. Melbourne was certainly a bustling town, and she could barely recall her early life here, only remembered that she was always scared at night, for her room was very dark and the noise from a nearby public house late into the night was often so loud she would have to put her pillow over her head to block it out.

The area where they lived was certainly not in this more elegant part of town. A twinge of remorse hit her then for not having more sympathy with her mother's plight. How hard it must have been for her to be thrown out of what was a safe place since she was a child and having to make her way into a harsh world. Was it any wonder she was eaten up with bitterness? If only she had been more open and discussed such matters with Faith. But it was too late for such thoughts now.

Chappie had driven the carriage through similar gates as the other houses, and they were now stopped in front of a door, certainly not as splendid as some they had passed. The double story house loomed up into the darkening sky, and the garden seemed to possess one large tree and a few shrubs but little else as far as she could tell. Polly had told her that the house was not in the centre of town, more towards the outer edges and not far from a river she called the Yarra.

A few disturbed birds kicked up a fuss in the tree where they were settling down for the night, when Chappie said, "Out you get, ladies." He offered a hand to Faith and then Polly. "Welcome, Faith."

She thought perhaps it should have been her father who made the welcome, but he had already entered the house and was talking to someone who she then saw was a bent old man as he came down the two steps and said a few words to Chappie. "That's old Tom," Polly said behind a hand to Faith as they went up the steps and through the door. "He does all the odd jobs around the place. Been with the family for years and barely says more than two words to me. I think he is scared of women." That was added with a small chuckle.

"Ah, welcome to your new home," Bryce Witherton said at last as they entered the candle-lit hallway. With a hand, he gestured for Faith to follow him into a room to one side of the hall. What she realised was a parlour was nicely furnished. Its two sofas, an armchair, and a couple of small tables were certainly of better quality than theirs at the lodging house, but by no means looked any different to those she had seen in other homes in Ballarat. "I hope you will be very happy here."

As he said that a boy came through the door and stood just inside it. His nightshirt proclaimed that he had left his bed to come and see the new arrivals. "This is my son James," her father said as he put a hand on the boy's shoulder and encouraged him forward. "Meet your sister that I told you about," he said, making Faith wonder why he had not also alerted her earlier to the fact that she had a half brother. She was beginning to think that her new-found father was somewhat strange—or perhaps simply shy.

"Do you like possums?" the boy asked, as he rubbed at his eyes. His hair was as black as night and so long that curls drooped over his forehead. Likely about ten, he bore no likeness to his father, so Faith guessed he had adopted his Mama's foreign colouring, for his skin was darker than most people's.

"Honestly, I know little about the animals. Perhaps you can teach me?"

"I'll let you look at my books. Just as long as you take care of them," he added hastily. "I treasure them."

"I promise." Smiling inwardly, she had a feeling she was going to like this strange boy, who seemed not one whit concerned that a sister had been brought to his home. It would take her a while longer to get used to the fact and to digest all the implications of having a sibling.

"It is late. I would like to retire," Polly stated. "Come Faith, I will show you to your room."

About to follow her, Faith looked more closely at the huge painting hanging above the fireplace. The striking woman wearing a gown of red with ruffles about the neckline was quite beautiful. "That's my Mama," James announced. "She lives in heaven. I think it is up there." He pointed to the ceiling, obviously unperturbed that his Mama was dead—or perhaps it had never been explained fully to him why his Mama was not around.

Faith stepped closer when she caught sight of the brooch adorning the woman's bosom. A gasp left her throat for there was little doubt it was her treasured gift from Polly. "Yes, it was hers," Polly, who had stopped by the door confirmed. Faith could not fail to see the odd look that passed between her and Witherton as she said this.

"Time you were back in bed, young scamp," her Papa said as he placed a hand on James' shoulder and ushered him from the room.

When they reached Polly's room, Faith turned to her and asked, "How is it that I am now the owner of that beautiful brooch? I do not understand. You said that it was a gift from your husband. Did you lie to me, Polly?"

"I will explain another time, Faith dear. Right now, I must get to my bed before I collapse with fatigue. Help me out of this confounded garment."

Faith knew she was not going to get a reasonable excuse from the woman at this time. It now appeared there were many gaps in the facts with which Polly had enlightened her. With a yawn she had to admit that she was also nearly asleep.

Later, Faith lay in the wide bed and stared around her, smiling despite her muddled thoughts. Their tiny bedroom at home that she had shared with her Ma would fit into this one about six times. She had left the candle burning in order to admire the furnishings. This room alone ensured she had no regrets now about fleeing. Pretty pink drapes framing the window, and matching bed hangings featured roses and small flying creatures. Her meagre possessions barely took up a quarter of one of the drawers in the dresser. There was even a tiny dressing table with three mirrors above it for her to see almost all of herself, something she had never been able to do before. Mind you, her tatty old nightie reminded her that she was no lady.

The most she could hope for was that all would be explained to her in due course. One thing was certain, her new Papa was kind and cared well for his son, despite the fact that he showed little interest in Faith, which made her wonder just why he had been so intent on bringing her here.

When she awoke hours later, the sun was already creeping through the window curtains and the candle had burnt out. In a hurry to get up and out into this new world she quickly used what Polly had told her was a commode, tucked behind a screen in the corner of the room, poured water from a jug into a small matching pattered china bowl and washed herself all over. She then dried herself on a towel she found hanging over the screen. The warmth of the water told her that someone had brought it in while she slept.

It seemed a shame to don her old skirt, but at least she had pushed a clean blouse, chemise, and pair of drawers into her bag. Pulling these on she then examined herself in the mirror as she sat on a small, cushioned chair facing the dressing table and brushed her hair using the nicest brush she had ever seen. It was part of a pretty set with a matching hand mirror, both decorated with small birds, enabling her to see the back of herself for the first time ever. Re-braiding her hair she then secured it with a length of silky ribbon she had found in one of the drawers of the dressing table. It seemed to be unused and so much nicer than her old ribbons.

A knock on the door that separated her room from Polly's announced that the old lady was awake and needed help. With light heart, she went in and assisted with her bathing and dressing. They then went down to the dining room that overlooked a small flower-filled garden at the back of the house.

Chapter Seven

Faith sat on the bench below the tree in the garden at the front of the house and watched a pair of brightly coloured birds arguing over a beetle one of them had picked up. James told her that the noisy birds were called parrots. Not only had he told her that, but he had produced one of what he said was his favourite books to show her a picture plus some details about the birds.

The tree offered shade from the early afternoon sun. James was at his lessons with Mr. Yates, a kindly gentleman who told Faith quietly that he despaired of the boy, who had little interest in anything but creatures. Polly was having her after luncheon nap, which left Faith with little to do but idle away an hour. If only she had heard word from Walt life would be so much more pleasurable.

She had given up expecting him to turn up at the door with an excuse as to why he had not followed her down. Her nights were filled with thoughts of all the horrible things that could have befallen him in the three days since they arrived here. Her only recourse now was to await a response to the letter she had penned yesterday and given to Chappie to take to the post office along with other mail written by her newfound Papa. She had seen little of that gentleman, and her curiosity was aroused further by Polly's non-committal answers to her queries. He seemed to spend a lot of time in his library, presumably taking care of his private matters. To own a big house such as this one he surely must have some sort of income, and Faith could only guess where this income was derived from.

"Having a rest?" Carrie, the tiny servant girl asked as she sat beside Faith and flapped a hand towards the noisy parrots as if to quieten them—which did not work. About fourteen years, she seemed to assist with just about everything around the house. It was she who brought Faith's warm water for bathing every morning—she helped Chappie's wife Edna in the kitchen and ran errands. In fact, she did most of the tasks Faith had performed back at home.

"Not really. But there is little for me to do while James is at his lessons and Polly is taking a nap in her room."

"Edna told me the Master found you up in Ballarat. No one knew he had a daughter. Caused quite a stir it did when he arrived with you along with old Polly. Did you know you had a Pa?" With a small laugh she patted Faith's knee, adding,

"Course you did, daft me, what I mean is did you know he was your long-lost Pa?"

"To be honest, no, I thought the man who was my Ma's husband—or so she said—was my Papa. It's been a strange time for me." That certainly was the whole truth.

"I bet it has." With a huge sigh Carrie nudged Faith on the arm. "I suppose it was a good sort of strange. I never knew my Pa. Ma told me he left us when I was born."

"Oh, I am sorry."

Carrie grinned. "Don't be. Ma said he was a straight-out bastard—her words not mine. Said he drank, bashed her, and then had the cheek to leave her all alone with me, a small 'un."

"Where is she now? I know you live here in the house so why don't you live with her anymore?"

Carrie's face twisted into a grimace. "Took off to Sydney Town, didn't she? Ran off with a sailor she met one night in a bar, so they told me. Left me with an old crone who brought me here when I was just a nipper."

Faith thought of her own problems, deciding she was not so bad off after all, at least her Ma had not abandoned her. Now she wondered if perhaps she was the one who had abandoned her Ma. "I'm sorry. That must have been hard for you."

Carrie laughed. "Don't be sad for me. It's a good house to live in, 'tis. I get a warm bed to sleep in, and plenty to eat." She patted her tummy. "And never really want for anything. We all have to work, don't we—unless we are born into the gentry. I get me clothes provided, and always get a new pair of boots every year."

"That's a truth, Carrie." Faith pondered on that remark, she certainly had not been born into the gentry, yet here she was now living what could be termed as a leisurely life. Mind you, that had its drawbacks, for she knew that soon she would become bored if she had no real tasks to do. Currently she felt as if she was floating between the old life and the new.

"What was your life like up there?" Carrie pointed off to nowhere in particular. "Didn't you have a Ma who cared for you either?"

Faith was unsure what to answer to that. Nibbling her lip, she shook her head. "I guess my Ma did care for me in a way as she never deserted me, but I was never sure just why she didn't leave me, for she didn't seem to have much in the way of love to give." Faith felt slightly ashamed to be admitting that, for there were many people who fared a lot worse than her.

"Funny old world, isn't it?" Carrie's attention seemed to wander, and Faith looked off to see what had captured her interest. The young fellow who she had been told tended to the garden was trimming with gusto at one of the shrubs. "Handsome, isn't he?" Carrie said, as her cheeks grew flushed. "I'm going to get Harry to marry me as soon as I am old enough." That remark was followed by a small laugh of what Faith thought was embarrassment.

"Yes, he certainly is a fine-looking man, Carrie." But not as fine looking as Walt, she added to herself. As she said this the man in question tossed his cutting tool to the ground and sauntered towards them.

"Hello ladies, mind if I sit a while with you. It's getting a bit hot out there in the sun." Without waiting for a response, he sat beside Faith, far too close in the small space allowed to him—so close that Faith could smell the aroma of sweat and soap that came from his body. Feeling uncomfortable, Faith shifted slightly away from him. Obviously unconcerned, he took his hat off, and wiped his brow with the end of the grubby kerchief he wore around his neck. He threw his hat down to the ground and his reddish-brown hair glistened with sweat that he swiped away with a finger when a droplet ran down his brow.

"There's more room this side," Carrie said, sounding aggrieved.

Ignoring that remark, he asked, "So how are you liking it here, Mistress Faith?"

"So far I am enjoying it, and you do not have to call me mistress for I am certainly not mistress of this house." Still unsure of quite where she stood in the scheme of things, she in fact currently felt more like a visitor. If only her new Papa would talk to her more, she might feel settled.

"But you are the master's daughter, so that should make you important for sure." He grinned, showing white teeth. His work in the sun had browned his skin and with his hair that was the colour of chestnuts he seemed quite foreign.

"I am no more important than either of you." Saying that, Faith rose. "I am sure Polly has finished her nap, so I must go and see if she needs assistance."

Instead of staying put, he got up too, which Faith could tell by the pout on Carrie's face made the girl more annoyed.

"I reckon the old woman will call you soon enough when she needs your help," he said.

About to say more to deter him, Faith looked toward Chappie who was coming through the gate, carrying what looked like letters. "Is there post for me?" she asked, with hope in her heart.

"Certainly is, Missy Faith. Arrived just this day." He handed the envelope to her and went on towards the house.

Even more eager to get away so that she could read the letter she saw was from Walt, she said, "I need to go to my room."

"Letter from a loved one?" Harry asked as he peered over her shoulder. "Did you leave him behind in Ballarat?"

About to tell him to mind his own business and get on with his chores, she heard Polly calling out, and without an answer to him she quickly went on towards the house. She heard Carrie call out to Harry but did not hear his answer. As fast as she could, she made for her room, deciding to ignore Polly's call for now. It was doubtful if the old lady's need was that urgent. To read Walt's explanation was far more compelling.

Sitting on her bed, she tore the message open, her heart thumping in her ears. Walt began with an apology for not following her when they left town, but his next words stunned her so much that for a moment the words jumbled together as her eyes misted over. It appeared that her Ma, on wondering where Faith was on the morning she left, went straight down to the store and demanded of Daisy Finch where Walt was. Mistakenly his Ma told her that Walt was leaving town that very day. Gert of course, presuming Faith was running away with him, went straight to where he was in the process of saddling his mare in the shed behind the store.

Polly rapped on her door, and Faith jumped up to answer her call. "Are you alright, Faith dear, you look quite ashen, are you ill?" she asked when Faith faced her.

With a small shake of the head, Faith said, "My Ma caught Walt as he was about to follow us and demanded where he was hiding me. Of course, Walt is no liar so told her the truth." She went and slumped down onto the edge of the bed, wiping at her tears.

"Oh my, so what did Gertrude do or say to that?"

Faith handed the page to Polly with a sob, "She is coming here. Told Walt how she didn't trust you or my Papa, and so once she gets help for Bertha at the lodging house, she is arranging a seat on the next coach."

Polly sat at her side and put an arm about Faith's shoulder. "Do not fret, we will tell your Papa and knowing Bryce he will have a solution. Anyway, she will not find anyone up there in a hurry to take on that task. Knowing Gertrude, she would not like to part with the wage they deserve."

"But what can he do? If she arrives, she can demand I return home. I know she will."

Polly looked to be thinking, then said, "I have a feeling that Bryce is within the law to decide he wants his daughter living in his home where you are most certainly better

132

off. Your Ma is an arrogant unfeeling person who can not say without doubt that she was a good mother to her only daughter. After all, she treated you no better than the lowest drudge. Look at you, your clothes are a disgrace. On that subject I forgot to tell you that your father has arranged for a seamstress to visit. Mrs. Hawthorn is due here later—she will see that you are soon wearing all that a young lady of your status requires."

Faith did not have an answer to that. Instead, she asked, "What will my Papa do when he knows she is on her way here to reclaim me?"

"Have no fear, he will know just what to do." Polly stood and patted Faith on the back. "You rest a while dear child and do not fear, Bryce will sort it out, I am certain of it. I will go and talk to him if he is free."

After she left, Faith went across to the window and stared out, seeing little. Not knowing enough about her father, she had no idea if he would fight to keep her here. The man was still a mystery to her. Walt was on his way; she must dwell on that good news and try to put what might happen when her Ma and Papa came face to face again out of her mind.

The arrival of Mistress Hawthorn at least gave Faith something else to think about. With an ever-smiling face the pleasant mid-aged woman measured and primped while talking non-stop for an hour about nothing in particular. When she left, Faith knew that at least six day dresses would be arriving soon, plus items of underclothing Faith had never thought to wear. With honest disgust she had cast an eye over Faith from her shoes to her hair, tutted endlessly and assured Faith that she would also need slippers, stockings, and boots along with outer wear and nightwear. Faith had an idea that the woman was so constantly happy because the bill for this vast array of clothing and accessories would be an amount that she could not imagine.

That night as she prepared for bed Faith sat at the dressing table and re-read the letter. Walt would probably arrive before her Ma as he was riding so would not be restricted by the coach's timetable, which likely had to make several stops. If Mistress Hawthorn kept her word, at least one of the day dresses and a pair of slippers would be delivered by tomorrow or the next day at the earliest, so Faith would look more presentable when he arrived.

Sleep refused to come and, when it finally did, her dreams were a mixture of gladness when she recalled the afternoon spent with Walt, and bewilderment when her Ma nagged at her and assured her that she was the worst daughter a woman could have.

* * *

"You look nice," Carrie said with what Faith suspected was envy, when Faith came down for lunch wearing the first promised new dress, with short puffy sleeves and a very full skirt. For the first time since her birthday when wearing the surprise frock that her Ma gave her, Faith felt something like pride in her appearance. Mrs. Hawthorn had assured her that she had no need for a corset, something Faith applauded. Just the thought of one was enough to make her feel nauseous.

The softness of the fabric of the bloomers beneath and the pretty lace trimmed chemise was heavenly, and when Faith looked down at her stocking clad feet in the soft slippers that matched the lilac flowers in the pattern of the dress, she felt like dancing.

"Yes, you look as pretty as a picture, Faith." Polly patted the chair at her side. "Come sit down and have something to eat. You missed breakfast this morning so must be hungry."

Earlier she had been too tense to think of food. Mrs. Hawthorn and her young helper tried on the two dresses that had been completed, deciding they were a perfect fit. Rather than eat Faith had been content to primp at herself in the mirror.

As Faith sat and Carrie placed a plate of ham and cheese tartlets in front of her, her Papa entered, rubbing his hands together, looking pleased with himself. He had not shared luncheon with them more than once since Faith's arrival and she wondered what had caused this special event. Mr. Yates, James' tutor accompanied him.

"You look delightful, Faith dear," he said as they both sat opposite her. "Did Madam Hawthorn do a pleasing job on your outfits?"

"Yes, indeed, and thank you so much for the gift." Faith felt a blush creeping up her cheeks. Should she call him Papa, or would he even expect her to at this stage?

"It is no gift dear girl. As my daughter, you are entitled to be dressed thus." Looking about he asked, "Where is young James?" When Mr. Yates replied that he had no idea, which was usual, her father began to tuck into his food, pausing to ask, "Are you settling in well? I must apologise for my lack of attention." With a wave of his fork he explained, "I am currently in the midst of business negotiations which take up most of my day." It seemed he was not about to disclose what this business was, and why should he?

While Faith wondered if he was going to broach the subject of her Ma's arrival, Carrie came back into the room then, looking flushed and harried. "James has answered a knock on the door," she exclaimed. "There is a gent there saying he is looking for you, Mistress Faith."

As Faith jumped up, James came in at a run. Beside him, tongue lolling and tail wagging was a bedraggled looking Bob. After one woof he headed straight to Faith and leapt at her, his front paws leaving a trail of mud down the front of her new dress.

"Sorry Miss," Carrie cried as she tried in vain to grab hold of Bob by the scruff of his neck. He simply licked her face which only made her more flustered.

Faith left the room at a near run with Bob on her heels. There at the door stood Walt, hat in hand, looking almost as untidy and travel worn as his dog. Without thought, Faith almost threw herself at him, arms outstretched. Realising how unladylike she was behaving, she stepped back and put her hands to her hot cheeks. "You are here," she said, knowing it was the silliest thing to say as Walt standing there was proof of his arrival. Suddenly remembering what had occurred with her Ma, she looked past him in anxiousness, breathing a huge sigh on seeing he was alone—apart from Bob, who was now licking James' face.

"What's his name?" the boy asked, getting to his feet. "Can I take him to the kitchen for a drink of water?"

"Thank you, that would be good, and he is called Bob." Walt said as he looked past Faith. Turning, she realised that the others had left the dining room and were now watching this scene with varying degrees of interest.

"Mrs. Pollock tells me that you are a good friend of my daughter's, young fellow, so am I to take it you have just arrived from Ballarat?" Without waiting for Walt's response, he added jovially, "You must be hungry. Come join us for luncheon and you can tell us all about your journey. Carrie, run and tell Edna to send another plate in for our guest."

Carrie ran off, followed by James and the dog. As the others went back into the dining room, Faith asked, "What did you do with your mare?"

"Some man who said his name was Chappie took her, saying he would take care of her. I think she will need a good rest and her hooves attended to. She served me well." Taking her hand, Walt turned Faith back towards him when she made to walk. "I am sorry about what happened with your Ma, Faith. I could not lie, for my Pa was there and he told her that I was off to Melbourne. As you may guess, he was not

138

well pleased with my decision to leave. Have you heard word from your Ma yet?"

Faith shook her head. "When do you think she should arrive? I am the one who should be sorry, Walt. I should have known that she would come looking for you."

With his free hand he stroked her cheek. "You look blooming, I take it everything has turned out well here, that is the main thing. Best worry about your Ma when she arrives—she could be delayed by all sorts of things. To be frank, I think she is acting foolishly—but it is not for me to say." Then, with a small laugh as he glanced at her mud-streaked skirt, he said, "I am so ashamed of my dog. It looks like he has ruined your nice frock."

"Oh, it is not ruined, it will wash up." As much as she treasured the garment it was now the last thing on her mind. "To be honest, Walt, I now have others and more on the way. My new Pa is very generous." Looking round to see that the others had returned to the dining room, she added in a near whisper, "But I am yet to fathom him out. He says little and spends sparse time with me or with his son James, so I have not had time to get to know him well."

"Perhaps he is simply not used to having a daughter around his house. Give him time Faith."

With a nod, she led him into the dining room. James was still absent, and Mrs.

Pollock was clearing her plate of food. "What are your plans, young man?" her Papa asked pleasantly. Mr. Yates rose and with a nod excused himself before walking out, likely in search of his wayward charge.

"My first stop after here will be my brother's house, where I will likely help him in the emporium he and his wife run. I am used to life in a busy store so it will be ideal employment for me. I do not know how much Faith has told you, but with the imminent arrival of her Ma with ideas of convincing her to go back to Ballarat, I will have to wait until I know the outcome before making any long-term plans of my own."

"Ah, Gertrude yes, now there is a woman it is not favourable to try and outwit. To be frank with the two of you, I am not surprised at her rash decision. The lady is set in her ideas and thinks her way is always the best." After wiping his mouth, he placed his serviette down and sat back. "As you say, Walter is it, we will await her arrival and see what eventuates."

To Faith he did not sound perturbed at all by this new turn of events and a notion hit her that perhaps he had thought this would be the outcome all along, and it was all a ruse to get her Ma to come to him. Carrie came in then with a plate of food for Walt, and while he ate, no more was said about her Ma's imminent arrival at his front door.

Mrs. Pollock retired to her room and her Papa to his library, leaving Faith and Walt alone. "Shall we go into the garden where we can talk?" Faith rose, and Walt took her hand. As they went outside Bob came bounding after them. James had likely been dragged unwillingly back to his lessons by Mr. Yates.

Faith led Walt to the shady seat beneath the tree as Harry appeared from around the side of the house. Seeing them, he sauntered across, removing his hat. "'Tis a fine afternoon for a visit," he said, as without invitation he sat beside Faith and nodded across her to Walt, asking, "Just arrived in town, have you?"

Faith curled her fists and glared at him, both of which he seemed to ignore as he prattled on about Melbourne. Wondering just how she could get him to go away, Walt saved her by saying mildly, "Yes, I have recently arrived and would really like to spend some time alone with this lovely lady, if you would be so good as to leave us. Perhaps you have work you should be attending to."

This did not please Harry at all. Without another word he glared at them both before walking back to where he had come from. "And just who is that impolite fellow?" Walt asked. "Not another member of this family?"

"No, he is just a worker here—he tends the garden. I have found that my Papa's laxness in giving orders to the staff has resulted in them thinking they can do and say whatever takes their fancy." Sadly, that was the truth, and Faith wondered at times how the house ran so smoothly.

"So, tell me what you have been doing since arriving—apart from being decked out in fine clothes." This Walt said with a smile as he ran a finger across the muddy stain down the front of her frock.

"Quite honestly, I have done little. I have concluded that I do not like lazing about idly. Mrs. Pollock seems to have brought me along with her under false pretences, for apart from helping her to bathe and dress and then undress at bedtime, I do little else for her. She could easily employ someone to do these simple tasks for her." Faith sighed and leaning closer said softly, "Between us I am also puzzled as to what she does for my Papa apart from some obscure matters to do with ledgers, which I have no idea about."

"It is so strange that neither of them told you about his marriage and his son before you made the decision to leave."

"I have something to show you." Taking his hand she pulled him to his feet, led him back to the house and along into the parlour. Pointing to the picture of James' mother she said, "That is Zelda, the

142

Spanish woman that it seems his mother forced him to marry. The poor unfortunate lady died while giving birth to James."

Walt moved closer. "Is that not your brooch that she wears, the one given to you by Mrs. Pollock?"

Faith nodded. "Another odd thing. Mrs. Pollock, Polly as she now wants me to call her, told me the piece of jewelry was given to her by her husband." Shaking her head she added, "Another odd piece in this puzzle that I cannot get an explanation for."

"Does seem odd. Looks like the pair of them were intent on convincing you to leave your Ma and come here to live. Most important thing is, are you glad you made the move, Faith?"

Putting a hand to her mouth she took a moment to think on that. "Yes, I am sure I did the right thing—but I must confess, Walt, on looking back, I think I would rather have run away with you." Heat rushed to her cheeks at that confession, but it was nothing but the truth. "I have lived my life so far amid nothing but lies. My Ma should have told me that the man I thought of as my father was not, and then this new man comes along claiming me as his daughter, and I find I am surrounded by more lies. It is distressing and stops me from enjoying this new life wholly as I guess I should."

Walt pulled her to him and held her close to his chest. "You have me Faith, and

I will never lie to you. I too wish that we could have run off together to make a new life for ourselves. But there is still time. Why not let us wait and see how things unfurl with your Ma and if you still want to escape, we will then decide what to do or where to go." He put a finger beneath her chin, tilted her head up and covered her mouth with a gentle kiss.

Chapter Eight

Faith sat at the small dressing table in her room and stared at her reflection as she brushed her hair. That kiss from Walt seemed imprinted on her lips and she ran her tongue across the bottom one, recalling how sweet it was. For a long time after releasing her he had looked into her eyes without speaking as he stroked her face. Carrie had appeared then, and the spell woven between them was broken by her silly nonsense chatter. Walt decided he had best get going to his brother's house, promising to come back tomorrow.

"Is that your beau?" Carrie had asked after he left. "Did he follow you for he cannot live without you?"

Without thought, Faith replied, "Yes, he is." This answer seemed to please Carrie, and Faith presumed that was because she now knew that Faith was not interested in Harry's advances.

Then Harry had sauntered towards them, a sneer on his face when Carrie told him that the newcomer was Faith's true love come to claim her. Faith left the silly pair to their nonsense and went back to the house.

Polly's call signalled that she was in need of assistance into bed, so Faith quickly fashioned a braid in her hair and went next door. Once the old lady was settled beneath the sheets, she patted the bed at her side saying, "Sit here and tell me all about your nice friend. He seems a likeable chap."

Obeying, Faith straightened her grubby frock and said, "Walt is the nicest, kindest person I have ever met."

"And did he say when your Mama is likely to arrive?" Her mouth˙narrowed as she said, "That woman is set on causing you more heartache, child. Please tell me you will not let her talk you into returning to Ballarat with her."

Not knowing quite how to respond to that Faith simply shook her head. Perhaps she was foolish, but deep down knew that her allegiance should be to the mother who had never deserted her despite all that had befallen her. To change the subject, she asked, "May I ask how it is that you seem so close to my Papa, even though you were employed by him when you were younger—and how is it that you kept in touch with him despite marrying and moving away—and if it is not too rude of me to ask, how is it that you ended up with that lovely brooch that his wife Zelda wears in her portrait down in the parlour?"

With a huge sigh, Polly looked towards the window as an owl's hoot echoed across the still air. After a long pause she took Faith's hand and ran her own veined fingers across it. "So many questions. I suppose it is time that you knew at least part of the truth for it appears that your father is not about to disclose it to you. I was still in the house when he married that Zelda woman—a disastrous match if ever there was one. His mother thought her a fine match for him as she was said to possess royal blood. The only good thing to come out of it was young James. My husband and I left the house soon after as he could not abide working for the new Mrs. Witherton any more than I could."

Dropping Faith's hand, she crossed her arms as she leant back against her plumped pillows. "Mr. Witherton happened to meet me one day at the market. After enquiring after my health, and once I told him I was leaving for Ballarat with my husband, he seemed to be pondering on a question. Finally, he put it to me that I seek out your Mama's whereabouts and then pass this information on to him."

"Which means he always meant to search for her, and you gave him the opportunity to learn all about Mama and me."

"Quite so. It was all his idea, and of course he gave me the brooch to pass on to you should I deem you deserved it."

Faith rubbed at her forehead, not quite knowing whether to be pleased that her real father had sought her out after all these years—or whether to conclude that she had been tricked into leaving her Mama and coming here with him. "So your part in the whole thing was to convince me to come here and the promised position as your companion was all his idea."

"Quite so, but you have to admit, Faith dear, that your life here is a whole lot easier and more comfortable than it was or would ever be with Gertrude Boswell."

Not about to admit any such thing, Faith rose and said, "I will leave you now to sleep. Goodnight Polly. Sleep well." A thought hit her then and she asked, "That boy Harry seems to be very arrogant and intrusive. How is it that a gardener seems to have the run of the place and is allowed to be so impertinent?"

"Ah, yes, the boy came with Zelda. Of course, he was just a young 'un then and I think he was related in some way to her—a distant cousin's son or something. Being an orphan, and Bryce being so kind-hearted, he allowed him to stay on after her death on the condition that he worked around the place. Unfortunately, he thinks that small connection to the late Mrs. Witherton allows

148

him special privileges. Do not let the fellow disturb you, dear girl."

"Oh, I will not." As she went back into her own room, Faith pondered on the fact that here was just another puzzle that had unfolded in this confusing house. At least that explained his unusually dark colouring. As she shut her door, Carrie was at the dressing table and Faith felt sure she was in the act of closing a drawer. "Looking for something?" Faith asked.

Turning abruptly, Carrie looked like a startled animal as she said, "Oh, I was looking for your spoilt frock to take it down for a laundering and to see if we can get that stain out of it, but I see you have not undressed yet. Shall I come back later?"

Certain she was lying, Faith caught her by the arm as she made to hurry from the room. "Did you expect to find my garment in the drawer, Carrie?"

"What drawer? Oh that..." Pointing to the dressing table she added, "I was just looking at myself in the mirror, not doing anything I am not allowed to do, honestly. You are so lucky to have such a pretty room."

Before Faith could add anything more, she left the room at a near run. Later, after Faith had changed into her new nightgown—a beautifully soft garment with lace trimming at the neck, hem and cuffs, a knock heralded the return of Carrie, who

149

said little apart from that she had come for the soiled frock, before leaving Faith to her thoughts.

Most of what Polly had disclosed was what Faith had already surmised. It had all proved too much of a coincidence that Bryce Witherton had run across her Ma and her by accident. It seemed that the plan the two of them concocted had worked satisfactorily for here she sat in his home.

Suddenly remembering how she had come upon Carrie perhaps rummaging through her possessions, Faith opened the drawer. All it contained were her new underthings and stockings, and a few beautifully embroidered handkerchiefs that Mrs. Hawthorn said were a special gift for her as she didn't seem to possess such of her own.

Faith surmised that likely Carrie was simply jealous of all these new things Faith had gained in her short time here. Still far too excited about Walt's arrival to settle down and sleep, she forgot all her worries and thought instead of him and the two of them going away together at some future time. At last, with these pleasant dreams, she finally fell into a peaceful sleep.

* * *

"How is your brother faring? I expect he was pleased to see you." After walking for a while as it was a pleasant morning, Faith and Walt sat on a bench in a small patch that had been set aside as parklands away from the hustle and noise of the city. She patted Bob who sat near her feet.

"He and his wife are enjoying their new daughter, Bridie. They are somewhat relieved that I have arrived at this time when she needs to spend her days with the baby. George hopes I will help in the store—and I have agreed. After all, I am used to it as it is how I have spent my life so far." He stared off for a while as if in thought and then added, "But I long for something more, Faith. To be honest I am bored with the occupation and long for something new."

A pang of remorse struck Faith at the sadness in his remark. Perhaps it would have been better by far if the two of them had run off together. Too late for such thoughts now. "I feel to blame for your dissatisfaction, for if I had not taken my father up on his offer perhaps you might have eventually set out on your own to search for a new life."

Walt put an arm about her shoulders and pulled her closer to his side. "I would never have gone off alone, dear girl, but would have tried to convince you to come with me."

"Well, there you are—for instead you came with me." As he stroked her arm they sat in silence, and Faith recalled the afternoon when they had discussed running off to start a new life elsewhere. "Where would you have headed had you not followed me here?" she asked.

With a shrug, he said, "I had not thought that far ahead. I did read about Adelaide and its surrounds a while back, and had a yen to head there, but it is a long overland journey, Faith, and would take many days. Anyway, life has a way of turning our plans around in such a way as they never seem to work out quite as expected so I will let each day come as it will—at least for now."

"To be honest with you, Walt, coming here with my new-found Papa has not worked out at all as I expected. He is distant and always attending to his business, whatever that is. He has no time for his son, or in fact for me. I really do not know what I am here for. Polly needs little assistance, despite her saying she will need me. Carrie could attend to the tasks she expects of me. I am so used to filling my days with jobs and errands that I often feel useless." Faith sighed. "I guess that is what women who posses the status that comes with having a rich parent are used to but being idle does not suit me."

"What a pair we are," he said on a small laugh. "Both not truly happy with our lot in life. Perhaps we should do what we discussed and simply run away." He nuzzled her neck and Faith felt a tremble that the simple gesture brought about right down to her toes.

Much as she would love to do that, her sense of right and wrong would not allow it. "I would feel like a traitor. After all, I was not forced along on this escapade but made the decision myself."

They talked about other things for a while and then he said, "My brother and his wife Alice would love to meet you, and said I was to invite you to tea one afternoon, perhaps Sunday. Would you care to do that?"

"I should love to—and to meet their new daughter."

"Splendid. I will pick you up about two o clock. George will let me borrow his small cart."

Soon after, Walt escorted her home and as there was no sign of her Papa or Polly he left, and after going to the kitchen for a glass of cordial she went up to her room. Edna the cook, although a likeable woman was nowhere near as chatty as her husband and as she was in the process of showing Carrie how to prepare a pie, Faith did not linger in the kitchen as she would have done with Bertha, who she missed terribly.

With an hour at least before dinner would be served, Faith sat at her dressing table to pen a letter to Bertha who had not responded to the one she had sent off soon after her arrival here. No doubt she had been too occupied with the changes taking place in the lodging house by Faith's Ma's strange decision to come after her. At a knock on her door she called, "Come in," hoping it was not Carrie who was becoming a nuisance with her endless silly chatter, mainly about the worthless Harry.

James poked his head around the door, asking, "Is it all right? I am not interrupting you, am I?"

"Of course not, silly boy. Come over here and tell me what you have been doing at your schooling. I do hope you are not causing Mr. Yates too much of a problem."

Faith turned her chair about and gestured to her bed. When he was perched on the edge he said, looking slightly pleased, "Old Yates is moving on. Says he is wasting his time here with me and so is off to teach three children that deserve his talents more than I."

"Oh dear, did he really say that to you, James? And what will you do now? You must learn your numbers and letters. Knowing the strange life cycle of a kangaroo will not serve you well as an adult."

He laughed aloud at that, for she knew it was precisely what he was more interested in than learning about other countries and how to add and subtract. "No silly, I heard him tell Papa that he had an offer to go to take charge of the family of a man who worked for the Government. Very important man, so he said. Papa was not pleased but I am very happy." Jumping down he then ran from the room.

Faith stared down at the half-written letter as an idea formed. She would wait and see if her Pa employed a replacement for Mr. Yates and if not, would offer to teach James all she knew which, although not extensive, would serve the boy well until he neared an age when he could go off to the University. If he agreed, it would help to ease the boredom of having little to do each day.

At the dinner table, as luck would have it, her father joined them, so Faith said, "James tells me that his tutor is moving on."

"Yes, that is so, and I am not well pleased." With a shrug he went on, "But now I must find another suitable tutor for him." He scowled across at James as if it was the boy's fault.

"Well, if you have trouble finding a replacement for him, I would be more than happy to take on the task. I am not a teacher by any means but know enough about basic mathematics and letters to ensure he does not squander his time with his books on the life structures of creatures."

For a moment he seemed to be pondering her suggestion, but then he asked, "So how is it that you are so skilled in these matters? Most young women are more interested in embroidery, dancing, and pretty outfits."

Almost laughing at the possibility of her Ma teaching her any of those ladylike pastimes, she said, "I did not attend school or have tutors, but my Ma taught me well, for she had the good fortune to share her lessons with the son of the house where she lived." It occurred to Faith then that of course he was the son she had shared her lessons with in his parents' house, where she lived after coming to this country with them as a twelve-year-old. No doubt a bond was formed between them as they grew into adulthood.

The same realisation must have struck him too, for he suddenly seemed confused. After a small cough that she took to be of embarrassment, he began to eat his dinner without further comment.

Determined not to let the subject go unanswered Faith asked, "So what is your answer? I would be pleased to share time with James." She smiled across at the boy, who seemed unconcerned as he ate his meal.

"Well, perhaps it would be fine—until I can employ a replacement." Wagging his fork towards his son, he added, "But do not think you can take advantage of your sister, James. You will pay heed to all that she tells you. And enough of the nonsense about wild creatures. It is past time that you were preparing for advanced education."

"Yes, Papa," was James' only response.

After they had all left the table, Faith went in search of Chappie to ask him to take Bertha's letter to the Post Office. As luck would have it, he came through the front door as she was about to go out. "Ah, Missy Faith, I have mail for you."

When he handed it over, Faith was overjoyed to see it was from Bertha, so said, "Oh, I will read this before sending mine back to my dear friend for I do not want to repeat myself." Going out to sit beneath the tree in the garden, she opened the message with excitement, eager to see what Bertha had to say about her Ma's departure.

Her excitement soon faded when she read the first paragraph. It seemed that her Mama had left Ballarat the same day as this letter, which meant her arrival here was imminent. Bertha was not happy with the people that Gert had left in charge of the lodging house and had left to find better employment. A husband and wife had taken the reins and the woman was a harridan of the worst kind who treated Bertha no better than the lowest kitchen maid. Luckily, she had found work with a very nice man who had recently lost his wife to sickness.

Faith sat staring at nothing as she pondered if she should go straight in and tell her Papa to expect the arrival of her Mama. Rubbing her forehead where an ache was forming, she knew she dreaded her Ma's coming. Going instead to find Polly, who was in the sitting room reading the daily newspaper, she said, "My Mama should be here within a day or two. I received a letter from Bertha who told me that Ma left at the same time as the mail."

Polly pointed to the nearest chair, saying, "Come sit dear girl, and do not fluster yourself. Remember that you are now living in your true Papa's home and, in fact, as his daughter are the woman of the house."

"Why do I not feel as such, Polly? I know that as soon as she appears I will feel just as I did when I lived with her—no better than a maid of all work."

"Silly girl. I thought you had put that life behind you and embraced your new-found position. Be brave and face up to her, whatever she decides to do. She has no hold over you, and Bryce will know exactly how to treat her."

Faith had her doubts about that. Worrying her bottom lip she cried, "But will he? He does not seem to have a way with people, I have found. He has barely spoken to me since my arrival, you must admit."

Polly set the paper down and stood. "I will go to him now and let him know how the land lies. That way he will be prepared for her arrival at his door." With a nod she marched from the room.

Feeling as if she was walking on hot coals, Faith barely slept that night. Expecting her Ma's arrival at the door the next day, Faith breathed a sigh of relief when her Ma had not shown up and she was able to escape the house with Walt. Dressed in one of her new frocks, a pretty blue and white muslin creation with a layered skirt, long sleeves, and a rather daring neckline, she almost ran out to greet him when he climbed down from the driver's seat and faced her, saying, "You look very pleasing Mistress Faith, I feel quite underdressed beside you." This remark was accompanied by one of his cheeky grins.

Faith gave him a soft punch on the arm. "Get away with you. I look very much the same as always." Leaning close she added in a soft voice, "To be honest, I do feel overdressed, but my old and shabby skirts and blouses have been tossed into the fire, so I am left to wear these new ones." That was the truth. One day she had wondered why her wardrobe had been reorganised and on calling Carrie was informed that it was done on the orders of Polly.

Leaning close, Walt took a strand of her hair that now hung down her back, into his fingers and said, "And your hair looks delightful. Promise me you will always wear it this way from now on. It shines like silk."

A blush rushed to her cheeks at the compliment. Truth was, the soap she now used certainly seemed to make her hair shinier, or perhaps it was that she had more time to brush leisurely. Not about to tell him that she simply said, "Thank you," as she bent to stroke Bob who stood by patiently.

It did not take long to reach his brother's home, but on the way, she had time to tell him of Bertha's news. "So, your Ma could arrive at any time. I am surprised that she let Bertha go."

"I think it was more a case of Bertha being unable to work with the husband and wife who my Ma has put in command of the lodging house."

"That does not surprise me at all." As Walt pulled Matilda to a halt a man and a woman came from a house that from first view seemed to be similar in design and size to her Papa's house. The garden certainly contained many more flowers of every shade and size. "Ah, here they are waiting for us." He jumped down from the cart and came around to offer a hand to Faith.

After introductions were made, they went inside. George's wife Alice spoke with a lilting Irish accent as she showed Faith around the home that she was obviously proud of. The baby awoke as they sat down for tea, and Faith was allowed to hold Bridie, a delightful child.

"I have not had a lot of experience with babies," Faith said on a laugh when she had to hand the baby to her mother before her frock got spoilt.

"Babies have no manners. They tend to not care who they wet on," Alice said before she took the child away to the next room. George excused himself and followed her out.

"Would you like babies of your own?" Walt surprised her by asking.

"I have never really thought about it to be honest. I suppose it is every woman's duty to have children, so I suppose if I marry, I will then have babies."

"If you marry? I thought every young woman dreamt of marrying one day." Walt seemed quite shocked by her answer.

Faith wanted to take back her words which she had uttered thoughtlessly. Should she tell him how she had dreamt of being his wife one day and therefore bearing his children? It reminded her once again how ignorant she was of the simplest facts of life. "I suppose that is the way of it," she said instead.

161

For a short time, he simply looked at her and Faith wished she could work out just what thoughts went through his mind. "You must have considered what it would be like to have a man waiting on your every need," he said at last with another grin.

"I have yet to see a man who does just that, Walt. From my viewpoint it seems that most wives are there to wait on the needs of their menfolk."

"You must know that all men are not like this, Faith."

The return of his brother and Alice cut that subject short and the conversation dwelt on how she was liking life in Melbourne, until they left a young maid to clear the table and went into the adjoining sitting room. "But you are glad that you made the change?" Alice asked when they were seated.

Faith hesitated before answering that, for was she truly happy living in her Pa's home? It certainly had not turned out as she expected—but then, had she really been sure of just what she expected of life under his roof? "Life is certainly a lot easier," she said. "But he is a strange man, and his household seems to run itself. There is a young man who is his gardener, who seems to do as he pleases. I found out that is likely because he is some sort of relative of my Papa's wife who died in childbirth. Chappie who cares for the

162

horses is the nicest man but his wife Edna, who is the cook, does not totally share his pleasant nature. Then there is young Carrie, the housemaid, one I do not entirely trust." Faith sighed, realising she had probably disclosed too much, for no doubt they had little real interest in that household.

"But Walt tells us that you share a bond with Mrs. Pollock, who instigated your change of lifestyle."

"Yes, I do—but she also has lied to me, and I feel that a scheme was plotted between her and my Pa to get me here. And I am still unsure why."

"No doubt he simply wanted to claim his long-lost daughter," Alice said. The subject soon changed to the emporium George managed, and Alice invited Faith to come visit one weekday when she would be assured of finding something she would love.

That made Faith realise, not for the first time, that although she had been fitted out with a completely new wardrobe and lived a life free of the worries that went along with having to manage financially, she possessed no funds to call her own. They said their goodbyes soon after that. On the way home, Faith told Walt how much she had enjoyed their visit. "You are so lucky to have a family such as yours," she said.

"That I am, Faith." He seemed about to say more but they had reached their destination, so he pulled Matilda to a halt in front of her Papa's home. Before helping her down, he took her hand in his and pressed a kiss to her knuckle. "Always remember that I am not far away should you ever need me. Now that you know where George and Alice live, you can come there at any time."

Faith realised that in truth she would prefer by far to be living at his brother's home along with him and his family, but that thought was interrupted by the shrill voice of Gertrude, who obviously stood in the hallway. The door was wide open, so it appeared that she had only just arrived.

"Would you like me to come inside with you," Walt asked, a concerned frown on his face, but Faith shook her head.

"I think perhaps this is something I should face alone. If I know my Ma well, it is likely that your presence would simply add fuel to her temper."

"Remember what I said. I am always here for you." Saying that he pulled her close and pressed his lips to hers, before climbing back onto the cart and urging Matilda on.

Faith waited until he had cleared the gateway, swallowed hard, straightened her shoulders, and went towards the house.

Chapter Nine

"There you are girl. Go fetch your things for we are leaving this house," were the first words that came from her Ma's mouth the moment Faith crossed the doorstep. No words of welcome, no explanations of why she had followed her here, just her usual harsh words of dominance.

In that moment Faith hated her with a vengeance that was so unlike her that it scared her more than her Ma's wrath. Taking her bonnet off, she gave it to Carrie who stood in the hallway, a look of something akin to terror on her face. The girl turned and ran towards the kitchen. "I am not leaving this house and you cannot make me," Faith said, hearing a tremble in her voice as she raised her chin.

"Can I not? We will see about that, girl. This man..." She gestured towards Bryce Witherton who seemed lost for words. "...Is not your father and I don't know where he got the idea that he is. The man that you thought was your Pa was not either, of course that is the truth, but I lay with another."

As if suddenly coming to life, her Papa darted forward, took hold of Faith's arm, and dragged her across the hallway like a rag doll. "Are you mad, woman? We both know that I was the only one you dallied with. For God's sake, Gertrude, do you live in a world of fancy? We were not much more than children and knew little of the ways of the world, so pray tell me where you met another person." Waving the hand that didn't hold Faith, he continued, "You spent your whole life at my Mama's beck and call, so I doubt very much that you would have found time to dally with another man, let alone get yourself in child with him. And to be honest, just who was there in the household to dally with. Most men were old enough to be your father, let alone your lover." Releasing Faith he ran a hand through his hair—hair that already looked to have suffered from his agitation.

Faith moved out of reach of them and went to the far end of the hallway. Tears clouded her vision as she brushed fingers that shook across her eyes. Could her mother have concocted another set of lies? One uppermost thought filled her mind and that was a desire to flee as far away from these two people as she was able. The thought came to her that there was no place in either of their lives for her.

Polly suddenly appeared from the parlour and taking Faith by the arm went to pull her away from these two, but her Mama darted forward, grabbed Faith's other arm and screamed, "And as for you, you scheming old hag, take your filthy hands off my daughter. If not for your interference, my girl would still be beneath my roof where she belongs."

As if something cracked inside her brain, Faith shook free of them and stepped toward the still open front door. "I do not belong in your house, Ma, where I was treated no better than a scullery maid." She gestured to her Papa and said in the calmest voice she could muster, "And as well as I appreciate that you were doing the best as you saw fit to offer me a good home sir, I do not really fit into your household and wonder just why you were so intent on bringing me here."

That seemed to shock them and they stared mutely at her. "But I thought you were happy here, girl. Did I not provide you with all that a young miss requires?" Her Papa shook his head as if totally perplexed.

Certainly not all, for you provided little affection, was what Faith wanted to tell him, but instead she said nothing, just turned for the stairs and ran up to her room where she slammed the door. Standing with her back to it she chewed on her lower lip until coming to a decision. She would take Walt up on his offer and get out of this house and away from both her Ma and her Pa, who seemed to be suffering some sort of delirium. There was no place for her in either of their lives. Let them fight their battles without her.

As hastily as she could, she pulled out a few of her garments from the wardrobe and drawers and stuffed all that she could into the small travelling bag which was the only receptacle that she possessed. She already wore her new boots so also packed a pair of soft slippers. No doubt she could buy any other necessities with what she gained for the brooch. That was given to her as a gift, so she had little qualms about taking it with her. Hadn't Polly told her so when she handed it over on that fateful day when this was all set in motion?

Pulling the chair over to the wardrobe she reached up and felt behind to where she had secured the treasure. A ball of panic began to form in her stomach when she could not lay her fingers on it. Jumping down she moved the chair sideways and tried again. All she came away with was dust on her fingers. The scream that began to fill her mouth made her want to vomit.

There was only one person in this house who would be likely to covet her brooch and that was Carrie. The girl was of lesser height than Faith so would likely have to gain the assistance of someone taller to assist her. That person had to be Harry—who else? Faith jumped down, ran across the room and down the stairs. The hallway was now empty, but raised voices came from the parlour. Faith dashed into the kitchen where Edna was preparing the evening meal, apparently oblivious to all that had passed in the hallway. "Where is Carrie?" she shouted, uncaring if she sounded rude. "Where is that wretch of a girl?"

Edna shook her head, a look of astonishment on her face. "Last I saw of her she was heading out back." She nodded in the direction of the door to the rear garden. "What's she done now?"

Without answering her, Faith pulled the door open and ran outside. The garden was empty, so she ran to the stable. Chappie was preparing fodder for the horses. "Where is Carrie and have you seen Harry?" she demanded.

Chappie looked taken aback by her attitude, but she cared little. "Haven't seen the chit since she ran out earlier just after you returned. Last I saw of Harry he was heading towards the gate out front." He scratched at his head. "Now I come to think about it, the lad wore a slyer look on his face than usual. What's he done girl?"

"The pair of them have stolen something that belongs to me." Faith rubbed at the tears dampening her cheeks. "I am leaving this place, Chappie. Thank you for all your kindness." Looking around her in confusion she said, "I must go." As she ran off, she heard him call out but ignored it.

More agitated than ever before she took the stairs two at a time, pulled her cape around her shoulders, grabbed the bag that was so overfull that it could not be closed, picked up her small reticule where she had stuffed her hairbrush and other small necessities, and as noiselessly as possible with her cumbersome load went down the stairs.

There were no shouts coming from the parlour now and for a second she wondered if they had taken their argument outside. The hallway was empty so she went out as stealthily as she could, pulling the door shut softly behind her. Her breath came out in a sigh of relief when there was no sight of her odd parents in the front garden. Perhaps her Ma had killed Bryce Witherton in her anger.

The drive to George and Alice's house took Walt less than twenty minutes but before she had trudged for all of ten minutes Faith was so weary, she had to rest and take in a few deep breaths. A disreputable looking man wearing the filthiest rags she had ever seen, stopped, and stared at her from bleary eyes making Faith's heart flutter in fear. If he decided to steal her belongings, she would not have the energy left to fend him off.

"Moving house, lass?" he asked in a kindly Scottish accent, as he pointed to her overfull bag. As she shook her head, he seemed to sense her fear and added, "Got somewhere nice to go have ye? Me and me poor old missus got chucked out of our home not long ago and the worry of it all sent her packing, didn't it?"

"I'm so sorry," Faith managed to say as she picked up her bag as best she could and turned to carry on with her walk.

"I'll help ye if ye have a penny to spare, lass," he said, holding out a hand that looked as if it had not been washed in a year.

"I'm so sorry, sir, but I have not a penny to my name." Doubtless he thought that a lie.

"Ah, 'tis a wicked world we live in, isn't it, lass." With those wise words he trudged off in the opposite direction and she breathed a sigh of relief.

As she neared her destination dusk was beginning to darken the sky. What would Walt and his family think of her turning up at their door in this bedraggled condition at this time of the evening? More to the point, would they think her quite mad for running off in such a way? Sagging with relief she went through their gateway and dropped her heavy load on the step before pulling at the bell rope. As she did so, a small figure darted out from behind the gatepost and ran to stand beside her, a big grin on his face.

"James, what on earth are you doing here?" she squealed just as the door opened and Walt stood there, looking totally perplexed as he looked from one to the other.

"I followed you," the boy stated, quite unabashed, as he bent to stroke Bob who had run out to greet them. "I saw you leaving so decided to come along with you. I didn't like that lady who arrived, and I don't think you like her much either. Sorry I couldn't assist you, but I am not strong enough. Is this an adventure?" Faith noticed he carried a satchel, no doubt packed with his books.

"No, it is not an adventure—and you must go home right now." She tried to sound angry but was too worn out to show such an emotion. "I have nothing but what I stand with here, James, and cannot possibly take a boy with me on my travels wherever they may take me. Go home this instant before anyone notices that you are gone."

Seeming to ignore such an order he shrugged and grinned up at Walt who had not uttered a word yet. "You were going to teach me all my lessons, so how will I learn anything if you are gone? I do not like the tutor I saw my Papa talking to so when I saw you were leaving thought it a good idea to go with you. Where are we off to?"

"We are off to nowhere, I am off alone," she said through tight lips. Looking to Walt she begged, "Will you take him back please?"

"I'll only run away again," James said with another cheeky grin.

"You'd best come inside for now," Walt said as he bent to pick up her bag. "Alice will wonder why I did not let you in. We cannot discuss this further on the doorstep. What has happened, Faith? I imagine it is your Ma who has brought this about. Need I repeat that you are more than welcome. I admit I did not expect you with a travelling companion." He ruffled James' already untidy hair. "You obviously did not either."

Ushering Faith before him he then closed the door. George and Alice stood at the doorway into the dining room, where no doubt their evening meal had been disrupted by her arrival at this hour. "Faith," Alice cried. "Dear girl, what has brought you out at this time of the evening? Of course you are more than welcome in our home." Glancing at James, she added, "And just who is this little one?"

"This is James my half brother, and he followed me here." Faith sagged onto a chair and pushed strands of dishevelled hair back. As if sensing her distress Bob put his snout on her lap and made a small

173

whimper in his throat. "He must go home." Looking to Walt she cried, "I could not stay in that crazy house another night, Walt. I am so sorry for this intrusion but did not have anywhere else to go. That wretch Carrie stole my brooch with the help of Harry I believe, and it looks like the pair of them have made off with it. I must beg your help to try and find them. I have nothing else in the world of value." Knowing she wailed like a forlorn child; tears misted her eyes.

"Of course, I will help you track them down, but it must wait until tomorrow. You look far too weary now and need rest. As for James here, I can take him home in the morning if you wish." Rubbing at his brow, Walt added, "That pair must have been there on the day when you showed me the portrait of James' mother wearing the jewelry." With a deep sigh and a shrug, he ushered Faith into the dining room. James followed them and without hesitation sat at the table.

"James, come away and stand over here beside me," Faith ordered. Of course, he ignored her.

"He's all right Faith." Alice smiled down at the cheeky boy. "Perhaps you are both hungry. Have you eaten?"

"To be honest, Alice, I have no appetite, but I could take a drink, perhaps tea, if you have some. I do not wish to be a bother—I was just frantic to get away from that house as fast as I could."

"Of course. Now you sit and I will fetch a drink for you. And perhaps you can come along to the kitchen with me young James and I will find you something to eat."

"I didn't like that Harry at all, and always knew he was a bad 'un," James chose to tell them before going out with Alice.

George followed them, leaving Faith alone with Walt. Instantly he pulled her into his arms and pressed a kiss on her forehead. "My darling Faith, we will find where those rogues have gone fear not, and we will recover your precious brooch. I never did trust that gardener chap. And from what you told me, you did not trust the girl either. They will not get away with this, I promise you."

Faith lay her head on his chest and let tears fall, whether they were with tiredness or sadness at the way things had turned out she did not know. Alice returned with a small tray carrying a pot and cup and saucer, which she set down on the table. "Come have a drink, Faith. James is tucking into a pie our cook has given him. What a funny little chap he is."

Faith had to agree with her, but was so perplexed now at the situation, she wondered what they would do with the child. As she thought that, James reappeared at the doorway, half-eaten pie in his hand. "I just remembered something, and thought I should tell you," he said. "I heard that idiot Harry tell Carrie that they would be on the next mail coach to Geelong. They didn't know I was hiding beneath the stairway." Without saying more, he left them alone again.

Walt looked at Faith and smiled. "I will find out the time of the next coach in the morning. I suggest you get some sleep and at first light we will make haste and catch up with them. At least we now have a starting point. Bless young James."

Bless the lad indeed. Faith finished her tea and Alice showed her to a bedroom. "James can share Walt's room," she said. "Please think of our home as yours, my dear Faith. Try and sleep."

After she left, Faith rummaged in her bag, thoughtfully brought up for her by Walt, and found her nightdress. Fearing she would be unable to sleep after the events of the evening, sheer exhaustion must have caught up with her for the first rays of dawn's light began to creep across the room when she opened her eyes.

Once they had eaten a hasty breakfast, they left the house. George had kindly given Walt the use of his small dray. Realising that it would be impossible to leave James behind, he now sat in the back with Bob at his side as they waved their farewells and began their journey into the unknown.

"George ensured we would have enough funds to make certain that we would not starve, plus the small amount I have amassed of my own, we should manage," Walt said as they headed towards the outskirts of Melbourne. After Faith had gone to her bed last evening it seemed he had gone to the mail coach station to find out the times that coaches would be leaving for Geelong today and with luck they would not be far behind it.

"What will we do if they have already found a jeweller to trade my brooch for money, Walt?" she cried. "I am destitute and cannot expect you to take care of me and James. I did not think this through before making my rash escape."

Shaking his head, he touched her hands that were twisting in anxiousness on her lap. "If that is the case then we will simply take whatever they have."

"Oh Walt, what would I do without you, my dear friend?"

Faith could not determine the look he cast her way. "I told you, did I not, that I would always be here for you. This is a promise, not some false words." Saying that he urged Matilda faster as the buildings grew sparser and they said little while he concentrated on driving. How would she ever be able to thank him for his steadfast friendship? And how she wished that she knew more about men and their way of thinking. Did he see her as more than a friend—she still had no way of knowing.

James chatted away behind them to Bob, explaining the animals that they passed. The boy certainly knew a lot about the wildlife, even if he knew little about arithmetic and history. When they passed a group of sparsely dressed natives, he said, "That's the Wurundjeri people, Bob, they have been in these parts for thousands of years."

Amazed at the child's knowledge, Faith leant across and asked, "How is it you know such things, James? Where did you learn this?"

"It is in one of my books," he explained with a wave of a small hand. "Mr. Yates told me I should not be interested in these people, but I told him that he was wrong, they live here the same as we do. In fact, my book says they have inhabited this country for millions of years, but we white folk have only been here a short time."

What a strange child he was. Never having the guidance of his father did not seem to have harmed him, leaving him to form his own ideas. Perhaps he could teach her more than she could teach him.

"We should catch up with the mail coach soon if I calculated well," Walt said, bringing her thoughts back to her woes.

"And what if they are not on the coach, Walt? For all we know they did not even get passage on the early one."

"I offered a small bribe to one of the drivers who kindly told me who would be travelling and by his explanation Harry is sure to be on it. Not many men have hair of red and such dark skins. His foreign look may be his downfall."

How she hoped he proved correct. As this thought crossed her mind, she caught sight of a female figure at the roadside ahead. The woman appeared to be agitated as she spoke to a man who looked to be a wanderer by the swag across his shoulders. They had passed a few such as he on the road out of the city. A bolt of shock ran through Faith when she recognised the person as Carrie. Walt must have come to a similar realisation for he pulled Matilda back into a walk.

When they were close enough to see her face, there was little doubt that it was the maid, and she was now waving in their direction in what seemed to be obvious distress. As they neared her side she stepped forward and Faith could see what clearly looked like a bruise along her left cheek. Her hair hung around her shoulders in a tangle, and what looked like manure stained her skirt. As she realised who she had called a halt to, she seemed to shrink back in fear.

179

"What in heaven's name has happened to you girl?" Walt shouted as he hastily climbed down and went around to her side. The man slunk off towards the nearby trees, apparently not wishing to become further involved in the girl's woes.

"That scum Harry threw me out," she screamed. "As the coach driver slowed to let a mob of cattle cross our path, he opened the door and tossed me out as if I am rubbish." Brushing at her already filthy face, she added to its woeful condition.

"Well, perhaps you got just what you deserved," Walt told her. "And is the thief on his way to Geelong with something that does not belong to him, something that is the property of Faith here?" His tone contained not a shred of kindness and she shrunk back even more.

"I had nothing to do with it, honestly," she cried. "He made me steal the brooch. I thought he was going to wed me."

"You stupid chit, both for assisting him and for imagining he would wed you. Why, you are barely out of childhood girl."

"I knew he was not to be trusted, Carrie, but cannot believe you did not come to me when he asked such a crime of you," Faith said as she wondered just what they would now do.

"But I loved him," Carrie moaned as she wiped at fresh tears.

Walt turned and stood beside the cart, looking up at Faith. "What do you suggest we do with her Faith?" He looked along the road they had travelled and rubbed at his chin. "It is bad enough we now have the boy here to worry about. If we take her along too, what then? Already she has slowed us down, and for all we know it could all be some ruse that the gardener fellow cooked up to do just that and perhaps put us off his trail."

Carrie grabbed at his arm. "No, no, I am telling the truth. Please don't leave me here, I beg of you."

Walt shook her off and walked away a few paces. For all that the girl had betrayed Faith's trust in her, she knew deep down that they could not abandon a lone girl out here at the side of the road. She would never forgive herself if they heard later that something foul had befallen her. The road was well-known to be full of no-goods, thieves, and escaped prisoners and even bushrangers. With a sigh she said, "Walt, we cannot just leave her here. If we take her, we can let the constable take care of her when we reach Geelong."

Returning to stand beside the cart, he beckoned to Carrie and when she came to his side warily, with little ceremony he bundled her into the back beside James. Bob growled low and sniffed at her skirts suspiciously. "It's all right," James said. "He will not hurt you; he knows you have been bad." As she sat, pulling the bedraggled shawl she carried about her shoulders, he asked, "Why did you do such a horrible thing? Faith was always nice to you and now you don't deserve her help." Carrie began to sob woefully.

"That's enough, James," Faith scolded, but gently. "She has been foolish, that's all."

Walt grunted as he climbed back onto his seat beside her but said nothing more as he clicked Matilda on. They travelled in silence for a few miles before he said, "We have lost some time, but still may catch up with the mail coach before it reaches town."

Faith leant close and said low, "Walt, I fear I have led you into this awful dilemma. We now have two others to worry about, and I have not a penny to my name. If we cannot catch up with the thief and regain my one treasure, I think we must return to Bryce Witherton's house, and I must bear my Ma's wrath and do whatever she decides I must do."

"That I will not let you do, Faith. We have come this far, and I am a man who carries things through. If we cannot regain your jewelry, have no fear, we will not starve. We can take the chit to the nearest police and that just leaves James to worry about. I am strong and able to work, and so we will manage."

Smiling her gratitude, Faith sat back. Already feeling fatigued, she closed her eyes, dozing for a short time until a jolt woke her. Walt had halted the cart behind a dray that had apparently lost some of its load. The driver was steering his oxen to the side, but it took a while for he and his mate to clear the bales that had fallen. "Sorry matey," he called saluting Walt, as he drove on.

Hours seemed to have passed when Walt directed the cart to one side of the road saying, "I must let Matilda rest for a while, or we will not make it to Geelong before nightfall. There's a small creek over there where she and Bob can get a drink." Coming around he assisted Faith down. As if sensing her urgent need he said, "You can get some privacy behind yonder shrubs." He then helped James down and without ceremony put Carrie on the ground where she followed Faith to the directed bushes.

"I think he hates me," she said when they were out of his hearing.

"Can you blame him, you foolish girl? I am also not too fond of you at this moment. What possessed you to think for one moment that the stupid fellow would ever throw his cap your way, let alone consider you as a bride?"

Carrie nibbled her fingertip, looking close to tears as they made their way back to where Walt watched Matilda and Bob as both drank their fill. He then brought out a small package from the back of the cart. "Alice thoughtfully provided us with some bread, cheese, and beef. It will see us through to when we can purchase a proper meal. Unfortunately, she only prepared enough for two so we will have to share it with these interlopers." He cast a disapproving eye over James and Carrie. "If we cannot reach town before nightfall, we must pray that we find some sort of accommodation."

As Faith ate her share of the food she dwelt on her guilt. If not for her and her stupid wish to be away from that house and her Ma, he would now be safely back at his brother's house. That caused her to then wonder just why he was so willing to take this on for her. Was he simply glad to get on the road and off to an adventure or was there another reason? One thing of which Faith was certain was that she trusted Walt with her life and deep down relished the thought that he might possibly have done this for her because he shared her deep feelings. Once again, how she wished she knew more of men and their ways, instead of being a stupid girl who understood not one whit of what prompted men to do what they do.

Chapter Ten

As they prepared to get back into the cart, Walt lifted Matilda's feet one by one and examined her hooves. When he reached the last one, he reached into the cart and retrieved a tool from his bag. Blowing out a huge sigh he said, "I am afraid I misjudged my mare's ability to travel over thirty miles in one day." Using the tool, he prised out a small pebble from the hoof. "I fear we must rest her or risk the chance of her going lame." With a hand above his eyes, he peered into the distance. "There is smoke that probably comes from a chimney just off to the south on the road ahead. We will see if we can perhaps take shelter in the barn for the night." With another sigh, he said, "I am sorry, Faith, but I cannot risk it."

"That's all right Walt, your mare is most important. At least she has brought us this far, and I would hate to see her in dire trouble through my stupidity."

Taking her arm, he gently led Faith away from Carrie and James, and said low, "Never ever blame yourself for mishaps that have nothing to do with you, dear girl. And you are not stupid. Try and think of this as a big adventure as young James seems to be doing." With a small laugh, he added, "I cannot own that the wench's presence brings me any pleasure, but I like the boy and his way of looking at life. As long as we are together, Faith, and have each other, just let us enjoy this time together."

He then cupped her cheeks and pressed a quick kiss on her lips before going back to his mare. Stroking her neck he murmured a few words of comfort to her, then turned to assist Faith and then their interlopers onto the cart. As they neared what turned out to be a rough built shack just a short way off the road, the sun was beginning to sink towards the horizon.

A skinny dog twice the size of Bob came towards the cart full pelt, its teeth bared in a snarl, but thankfully was stopped in his stride by the heavy chain that held him fixed to a post. Bob gave an answering bark and Walt gestured for James to keep him beside him. Before Walt alighted, a woman Faith guessed to be of similar age to her Ma appeared at the door, wiping her hands on a filthy apron. After she sent a shrill order to the dog, it skulked back towards a box that probably served as its only shelter.

A small boy clung to her skirts, a thumb sticking into his mouth. "Forgive our intrusion, Madam," Walt said as he doffed his hat. "Would you be kind enough to let us spend the night in the barn I see over there." The hat was waved towards the building that looked as if a strong wind would tear it from the ground. "Of course, I would pay you for your trouble."

Pushing the child behind her she slammed the door in his face and came towards them as Walt climbed down to face her. Peering into the cart she said, "They ain't yer kids, are they?"

"No, no Ma'am, they are simply relatives that we are taking to Geelong. My mare has a small problem, or we would have carried on until we were nearer the town to save her, so I would rather rest her for a night." Looking to the sky he added, "It looks like rain may be heading this way, so I fear we need to take shelter before darkness."

With a nod, she held out her right hand. "Give me five shillings and you can sleep there. There's water from the well out back. I fear I only have a small amount of lamb to offer you and perhaps a slab of bread each, and that'll be another five shillings. I ain't got no tea till me man comes back tomorrow with me rations."

Walt delved into his pocket and handed her the money. "Thank you kindly, Ma'am. We will be no trouble." Gripping the money, she turned and went back inside her house. "Come, at least we have shelter now," he

187

said as he helped first Faith and then the others down.

"Oh, Walt, she asked a lot of you for so little." Faith felt as if tears were waiting to fall.

"Nonsense. The poor woman looks as if she has little in the way of pleasures and needs the money more than I."

The barn, if it could be called such, proved to be more ramshackle than the house. A wind had begun to blow up and it whistled through the many cracks between the planks. Walt tethered Matilda a short distance away where there was a small patch of grass. After giving her a share of the grain he had brought with him, he then went off with the bucket for her water. When he came inside to join them, he let out a small laugh. "I fear we may find ourselves blown away should this wind get up, but we are under cover at least for now. Be wary of snakes who may well also be taking shelter."

At that Carrie let out a squeal. "What's that?" she squeaked, pointing to a dim corner.

James laughed. "Goodness, that's simply a spiny anteater. He is after ants— did you know that he can smell them under the ground? He is more scared of us than we of him." So saying he went to kneel near the creature which scuttled further into the darkness along the lower wall. Bob took a sniff of it but had the sense to keep his nose well clear of the many spines along its back.

Looking around, Faith wondered how any of them could sleep in here for there was nothing resembling a bed or even a seat. "There is plenty of dry grass and a small amount of hay here in the corner. We can spread that on the ground." Walt then began to kick the hay into a pile. "I will fill our water bag and then fetch our belongings. Perhaps we have some items of clothing that will serve as bedding."

Once Faith's cape and Carrie's shawl were spread on top of the hay and their bags set down as some sort of pillows, it in no way resembled a bed anywhere near her nice comfortable one at her Pa's house but was better than lying on the dirt floor. The woman came with what was indeed a meagre share of meat and bread for each of them. Eying their makeshift bed she said, "I'll fetch a blanket. It might get chilly overnight, especially if it rains."

After she returned with a threadbare piece of rag that could not remotely be called a blanket and then left, Walt eyed the cloth, saying, "That was kind of her." This he said with a grin and Faith had a sudden desire to laugh too. Carrie and James looked at them as if suspecting they had gone mad, and perhaps they had. Never in her life had Faith imagined spending the night in some remote and nameless place with this motley group. Somewhere deep inside she felt a pang of dismay that the two younger ones had intruded on this journey—and wondered how it would have played out should it have just been her and Walt as planned.

"At least it is a warm night," Walt said as they lay side by side. "Try and get some sleep Faith, for it has been a long and wearying day."

Wondering just how she was going to get any sleep with him so close at her side, she fidgeted. Bob lay next to her between she and James, and he snuffled a few times before both he and the boy were asleep. Carrie lay on the far side of James and after a few self-pitying moans she went silent. Wiggling her now bare feet, Faith turned onto her side facing away from Walt, but as he settled more comfortably , she could feel the warmth from his body.

A jolt of pleasure ran through her when his breath fanned her ear as he whispered, "Good night my love."

Stifling a small cough, she turned onto her back but then realised that their noses almost touched. Feeling very unsure of herself she asked, "Am I really?"

"Really what?" That was accompanied by one of his soft chuckles.

"You know—what you called me?" Now she felt even more silly and childish, for she felt sure he knew just what she asked of him.

"Haven't I made it clear to you by now that you mean the world to me, else why would I now be lying here beside you and not back home in Ballarat where I would be comfortably nestled in my own bed with a full stomach after eating a hearty supper."

Carrie chose that moment to make a strange noise in her throat, halfway between another sob or a cough, and Faith realised that the girl was not asleep but heard all that was said.

"Go to sleep," Walt said, as he put an arm about Faith's middle and pulled her snugly against him.

Faith relished the feel of his strong arm and then a leg as he seemed to snuggle closer. Was this how it felt to be wed to a man that you slept beside for the rest of your life, she wondered. Somehow, they seemed to fit together like pieces of a puzzle, and it felt so right. Certain that she would get no sleep this night, she awoke with a start when she heard a cock crow in the distance. Rubbing at her eyes she sat up, disappointed that Walt was not there. James had gone too, so she poked Carrie on the shoulder. The girl also sat up, yawning widely. "You are so lucky to have a beau who calls you his love," she said, proving she had overheard Walt's words.

"Some day you will find yourself a nice young man who will cherish you. Come now, we must prepare for the day. Walt wants to make an early start. I do hope that his mare is recovered and is not lame."

As it happened Matilda was already harnessed when they went outside. "You can refresh yourselves at the well behind the house," Walt said, sending Faith a small smile.

Carrie went off behind a bush and Faith took the small rag Walt handed her and walked to the well. She was drying her face when Carrie's scream echoed through the trees. Tripping over a small mound she raced as fast as she could in the direction Carrie had disappeared. The girl was holding her leg just above her knee and still screaming when Faith found her. "What on earth is wrong?" she cried going down on her haunches before Carrie.

"Something bit me," she squealed as she hopped on one leg.

"Not a snake, was it?" Faith looked about but there was no sign of a reptile of any kind. "Did you see where it went?"

"No, it was small. I think it was a spider. I bent to do my business and felt a sting. I didn't see anything."

"Perhaps the creature was just scared. Not many spiders are dangerous Carrie, so I heard. Come along, let's get on our way.

Walter is eager to get on the road as quickly as possible."

Taking Carrie by the arm she led the limping girl back to where Walt was waiting by the cart. James and Bob were already in the back. "A spider bit me," Carrie wailed.

"Don't worry, there are not many spiders that will kill you," James advised her. "If you start to feel a lot of pain, or feel sick, then you had better start to worry."

His sage warning just made Carrie cry louder. "What do you know?" she screamed. "I heard of someone dying only a while back from a serious bite."

"It says in one of my books that the worst spider bite was to someone up north in Sydney Town but those nasty things don't venture down this far. I think it might be too cold for them."

"Well, thank you for your advice, young James. But we must get on our way." Walt lifted Carrie and plonked her down beside James where she sat rubbing her leg and sobbing pitifully.

After assisting Faith up, he went around and clicked Matilda on. The woman had not appeared so there was no promised tea. No doubt her husband had not returned from his nightly foray. "How on earth do people survive out here, Walt. They had no cattle or sheep and not even a cow for milking. What do you suppose her husband does to keep his family alive?"

"We will never know. Perhaps he is a bushranger. Maybe we will pass him on the road going about his business."

But they saw no white folk, only a mob of natives in the distance as they covered the next few miles. After a while Carrie's sobs turned to low moans. "It looks a bit nasty and red," James chose to tell them. As he said that Carrie leaned over the side of the cart and vomited loudly. "I think she is ill," he added unnecessarily.

Walt pulled Matilda to a halt and leant over to hand Carrie the water bag. "Take a swig," he said. "It will make you feel better."

After she took a mouthful of water she vomited again. "What shall we do Walt?" Faith asked. "She really is sick."

"I don't think we can do much for her until we reach town. Are you cold?" he asked the girl.

"No, I am hotter than I have ever been. Am I going to die?" Her wail frightened Faith more than the vomiting.

"No, you are not going to die. According to my book, if it was what they say has a red stripe on its back, it will not kill you. Just make you feel poorly." At James' sage words she simply cried even more.

"All we can do now is get to town as fast as we can. I estimate we should be there in about an hour." Walt clicked Matilda on.

194

Faith had no way of knowing if it was an hour later that signs showed that they neared town, but to her it seemed endless as Carrie's moans grew worse, and her face grew more flushed. Walt pulled Matilda to a halt before a house at the side of the road that looked to be lived in and jumped down. A few minutes later he came back. "There is a doctor's house not far along the road up here, but the man said that the doctor is often off far and wide treating his patients. He advised us to keep going into town where we can find the new infirmary, and I feel certain that would be best."

On they went for a mile or so. Walt pulled up beside a group of men who seemed to be haggling over a parrot one held in a cage. After asking for directions to the infirmary, a couple of them pointed along and told them to keep going. "Can't miss it," one said.

They certainly could not miss the building, and soon after telling Faith to stay in the cart, Walt was carrying a still moaning Carrie through a door marked for emergencies. "I hope you are correct, James, and people do not die of spider bites," she said. His answer to that was a shrug.

After about fifteen minutes Walt came back out, without Carrie. "When I said she was no relative of mine but simply a girl that we had picked up at the roadside a young nurse told me to leave her there until a doctor was available to examine her," he explained.

"Shall we return for her later?" Faith asked, now feeling somehow responsible for the silly girl.

"It's getting late into the afternoon, Faith. I asked the nurse for directions to the mail coach station, and I suggest we head there next. If Harry was on the coach, there is no telling where he could be now. We have already let too much time pass." After climbing back and setting Matilda into a trot, he said, "I have been thinking that we should next find the local constable. Matilda must be rested, and we all need food and shelter."

When Walt pulled Matilda to a halt outside the coach station, the empty coach still sat there minus the horses. Three men were deep in discussion, or perhaps argument. One did not look happy. Walt climbed down and approached them and when he returned to stand beside Faith he rubbed at his eyes in obvious tiredness. "It seems that there was trouble not far out of town. A group of rogues halted the coach and demanded cash and valuables from the passengers at gunpoint."

The first thought that hit Faith was that the brooch was now in the hands of some bushranger and by now could be anywhere within miles. "Oh Walt," she cried. "Did they say what was stolen and more to the point did you find out if Harry was on that coach?"

"They said that one man refused to pass over his money and so got injured in the scuffle that followed. He is now in the infirmary along with a couple of women who were so distressed they had fainting fits."

"Did this man happen to look like the scoundrel?"

"Their description was somewhat vague, but they did say he was a young man who said little on the journey. I suggest we get back to the infirmary now and hope it was him, and also for your sake that he did not relinquish your precious jewelry."

At that moment Faith felt close to a fainting fit herself. "When will anything go right for us?" she moaned.

"If I know Harry he will not have parted with your treasure, Faith," James chose to announce.

Walt climbed aboard, turned Matilda around and into a trot. Darkness was not far away as they pulled up in front of the infirmary. Walt lifted Bob out and then James who complained that he wanted to wee. "Keep an eye on Bob please, young fellow, and whatever you do keep out of long grass and away from fallen logs. The last thing we need now is for you or my dog to get in trouble. And then come right back to the cart and watch over Matilda."

James nodded and then scampered towards the nearest tree with Bob at his heels. Walt assisted Faith down, and they hurried inside where a different nurse was now in charge. Walt explained to her that they had brought Carrie in earlier and she directed them to a ward, saying, "The girl can probably go home soon." As she walked away, she sighed as if tired—or bored.

Walt took Faith by the hand. "Never mind about Carrie. There does not seem to be any other member of staff about so we will go through the wards and see if we can spot the scoundrel. If stopped, we will say we are looking for Carrie."

After scanning the beds where patients lay in differing positions and obviously with differing conditions, they did not see a young male with reddish hair. Faith had never felt so tired or forlorn in her life. The nurse who spoke to them earlier came marching towards them, demanding, "What are you doing here? These patients are very sick. The female you are looking for was in a room near the entrance, but it now appears that she has left the infirmary."

"Left?" The word came out of Faith at almost a squeal. "How could she leave, she had nowhere to go, and we were the only people she knew in these parts."

The nurse shrugged with indifference. "I think she may have left in a hurry. I was told that she went after the young fellow who came in earlier with an injury to his leg."

"That was not the man who was injured in the stagecoach when it was held up, was it?" Walt asked, as Faith felt sick inside, guessing it was almost certainly Harry.

"All I know is that the girl saw this man as he was about to take himself out of the infirmary, against our wishes, and in a hurry—a small quarrel followed, and then she ran after him. It is no longer our business what either of them do."

Faith sank onto a nearby bench, her head in her hands. As if from a distance she heard Walt ask directions to where he could find the local police constable. The nurse said something, but her words came to her through a fog of tiredness and wretchedness. What possessed them to start out on this stupid chase?

Chapter Eleven

"Don't worry, Walt will find them," James said as he tucked into the food a young girl had delivered to the room they were all going to share for the night. What made James so sure she had no idea—she had just about given up the thought of getting her precious brooch back and was now wishing she had never been given it or met Mrs. Pollock.

After ensuring they were comfortably settled in a small lodging house that the constable had recommended, Walt had eaten his meal in a hurry and gone back to check that Matilda was comfortable in the small yard behind the inn. Bob lay on the floor near her feet, snoring contentedly now that his belly was full. Faith's new fear was that Walt would run out of money, despite him reassuring her that they would not starve or be without a warm place to sleep in the foreseeable future. But how long that foreseeable future would be, she could not contemplate.

Sleep evaded her despite being more tired than ever before. As dawn began to send streaks of light across the sky, Faith put her feet to the floor and yawned. The third narrow bed in the room had not been slept in. Even though she had barely closed her eyes, she still cherished a small hope that Walt had crept in sometime during the night. After a soft tap on the door the girl who had brought their meal last evening entered and cheerfully bid them a good day as she set a jug of water on the washstand.

Faith quickly washed and dressed before giving James a soft push. When he sat up, rubbing his eyes, she said, "Get dressed while I take Bob outside. I will ask the owner if Walt returned during the night." There was a small chance that he might have slept elsewhere so as not to disturb their sleep.

The owner was nowhere to be seen but a boy was sweeping the floor of the entrance hall and to Faith's query he shook his head. "Nobody has come and gone to my knowing, miss."

Her next thought after using the outhouse was to check the yard where Matilda had spent the night. She whinnied softly when Faith called her name and came to meet her at the fence. "Did your master come to see you during the night?" At her question, the mare nudged her arm. Faith then went to the shed where Walt had left the cart and all the harness, a fear growing in her that it might have been stolen to add to their woes. Luckily it was all there, so she quickly scooped up a small serving of grain and took it back to Matilda.

Leaving the mare munching contentedly, she chewed on her lip as she mulled over what to do next. Perhaps the constable would have news. As that was the only idea she had, and with Bob at her heels, she marched down to the police station, which luckily was not far away. A constable of mid years sat behind a desk and looked up with disinterest as she entered. "Do you recall the man who came in yesterday looking for a scoundrel named Harry? My friend's name is Walter Finch, and he was trying to find this Harry who made off with a precious piece of jewelry belonging to me. A young girl might be travelling with him. He was injured in the attack on the mail coach."

The man's response was to shrug his huge shoulders. Looking down at what was obviously some sort of ledger he then said, "Ah yes, I see it is marked here, but I was not around when he came in so have no idea about your young man." With a podgy finger he traced the writing in the book and added, "It says that a constable told him a search would be carried out, but the man went off on his own accord without waiting for assistance."

Faith rubbed at her now aching forehead. "And did any police set off to search for this person after Walter left?"

"You can be sure a search will be carried out, but as we have no idea what direction he left in, it will take some time to track him down. We will likely use our native tracker."

A scream welled in her throat as she told him where she was staying. "I would be pleased if you can let me know if any progress is made on finding this Harry person, and I will await Walter's return." Leaving him with a bored look on his face she returned to see how James was faring.

The boy was dressed and together they went down to the dining room. "So, Walt has gone off in search of Harry and Carrie," he said. "But how will he know where they have gone?"

That was exactly what had been niggling at Faith. No doubt Walt knew what he was doing, but now she had another fear. Unarmed and, as far as she knew unskilled in tracking, what had possessed him to go off on what she saw as a wild goose chase. As answer to James she said, "Walt knows what he is doing. Have no fear he will be back soon with Harry in tow." To be honest, she sincerely hoped never to set eyes on the Spaniard again, just as long as Walt returned safely. By now she cared little if he brought her brooch back, for she hated it intensely. The stupid piece of jewelry had caused more problems than it was worth.

Three days passed in wretched anticipation with still no sign of Walt. After yet another fruitless inquiry of the constables, she said to James, "I fear we will run out of funds if we stay here any longer, James. I have been thinking that we might do well to return to Melbourne."

"What, on our own?" the boy squeaked. "I don't know how to drive a carriage or cart. And anyway, I have no wish to return to that house." He plonked himself down on his bed and put his chin in his hands.

"I have been watching Walt, and how hard can it be?" Deep down she was terrified. What if they were met by bushrangers who stole the small amount of money remaining from what Walt left with her. "We have no other option, James. If we run out of money and Walt still does not return, what would we do?"

"We can work. That boy who does jobs around this place is not much older than me. And you told me that you worked in your Mama's lodging house before you left for my Pa's house."

That was a fact, Faith mused. But truth was, she did not relish working like a slave in some lodging house for meagre wages. Then the thought hit her that she had become a spoiled miss who thought that working was beneath her. "All right, we will search for positions, perhaps in a rich man's residence, but if Walt does not return soon, we will have to return home."

"Good. I will be a good worker, I promise you." With a finger beneath his chin, he added, "Perhaps I can get a job with someone who treats animals. I know a lot about creatures."

"That you do, James. We will buy a newspaper and look through the offers of work, but should Walt fail to return we have no other option but to go home." As she said the words, she felt sick with despair. Why had Walt gone off like that, and more to the point how could he leave her alone without a word of explanation? Surely he knew that she would be in a terrible position as well as fretting continually on how he was faring. As James had said many times, this was a huge country and people got lost out in the bush all the time. The natives seemed to be the only folk who knew their way around this vast land as they spent their days wandering.

"Let's say we give it a try. What do you think—if we do not earn any money within…" He gave that a moment's thought. "Perhaps a month."

"A month? We will end up begging for money on the street if we do not find employment soon." It occurred to Faith that this boy probably had more sense than she would ever have. And his common sense had come naturally, for he most certainly never had a good person to teach him the hard facts of life. "A week. We will give it a week. But come, we must start right away."

With Bob at their heels, they headed for the nearest shop that sold newspapers as well as tobacco, pipes and all the other stuff that men seemed to find interesting. In fact, a few men lingered outside the shop and eyed Faith with unwanted interest as she sent James inside with a coin in the hope that it was sufficient to buy The Advertiser. "Need any help missus?" one of the scruffier of them asked loudly and a couple of others tittered.

"No, thank you kindly," she answered primly, and the moment James came back out she took him by the arm to hurry him away.

"What did they want of you?" James wondered, and Faith chewed on her lip as she wondered indeed what they wanted. Already missing Walt she then realised that she must get used to life without his watchfulness and the sense of security he gave merely by his presence.

"Nothing, they were being silly," she retorted, realising that a blush reddened her cheeks, probably brought on by indignation.

They hurried back to sit on a log near Matilda's yard. The mare knickered in welcome and came to put her head over the fence. "I expect she is wondering where

Walt is," James said as he stroked her nose. "I know Bob is worried too."

Not half as much as me, Faith thought as she opened the paper and began to use a finger to go down the page of employment opportunities. "This looks like a possibility," she said as she stopped by one that announced that someone was looking for a chaperone for their two young daughters. As it did not state what age the girls were, Faith hoped they were small and shy.

The house they were directed to was unimpressive and faced the bay, which was rather nice. Faith took James by the hand and together they climbed the two steps and she pulled the bell at the side of the door. It was opened by a tall woman who looked to be of similar age to Mrs. Pollock. "And what can I do for you?" she asked in an accent that Faith recognised as Scottish.

"I am applying for the position advertised in the newspaper," Faith said in a clear voice that she hoped did not show how nervous she was. "And James here is my brother, who is willing to work at anything."

"And how is it that you are here alone with such a small laddie at your side who looks far too young to think of working for a living." This was said in a friendly manner which gave Faith encouragement to continue. At least the door had not been slammed in her face—yet.

"Our parents have recently died and left us alone to fend for ourselves." Fingers crossed behind her back she hoped the lie was believed. "We find ourselves destitute and must therefore seek employment or starve." Another almost whopping lie.

The woman, obviously the housekeeper just shook her head, and tutted, hopefully in sympathy for these two orphans. Pointing to Bob she asked, "And does the animal seek employment also?"

Obviously, the woman had a keen sense of humour for not many folks would ask such a question. "Bob is the best-behaved dog you will find," James told her as he stroked Bob's head. "He is a good ratter, and you will never have to worry about another mouse while he is around, miss."

"Hmm, well, come along in, and I will tell the mistress that you are here." Opening the door wide she beckoned them inside and then to a room to the right of the small hallway. It was a parlour, not lavishly decorated, its furniture well-worn. "Take a seat." She made no comment on Bob who had followed them in—a good sign, Faith thought.

"She seems nice," James whispered when she had left them alone. "She has a funny way of speaking."

"That's because she comes from Scotland. You know where that is do you not? It sits above England on the map."

James nodded as he looked with interest about the somewhat shabby room. "I don't think they are rich," he murmured. And Faith shushed him, even though she agreed with him.

After a few moments the woman returned, beckoning to them. "Come along with me, Madam will see you now." Glancing down at Bob she added, "I suggest you leave him down here for now. I will take him to the kitchen and give him some of our left-over meat."

A large tabby cat sauntered from the back of the hallway as they followed the woman up a flight of stairs. It hissed at Bob, who simply ignored it as he watched them ascend. The woman opened a door to one side of the landing and ushered them inside. "Here they are Madam," she said, then left them standing just inside the door which she closed. The room was overly warm, and Faith wondered if they had found another Polly who seemed to relish a heated room.

"Come closer," the lady said in a clear voice. "Let me look at you." She waved them nearer, and Faith put a hand on James' back as they obeyed. Lying on a chaise, she looked to be not a lot older than Faith's Ma, the blanket across her knees proving that she might have some problem with her legs, for she surely could not be suffering from the cold. "My housekeeper tells me that you are both seeking employment. I am so sorry about the loss of your parents. You must be suffering in your bereavement." Faith's insides did a somersault and her guilt almost made her blurt out that she lied. "I am a recently widowed woman so understand such pain. Now, please sit down and tell me what you are proficient at, and I will see if there is a place in my household for you."

Faith sat on a small chair and James on a stool near her side. "I am skilled at running a household. I have been teaching young James his arithmetic and writing for some time." Another lie, for they had barely had time for lessons. "He is willing to work in the garden, fetching and carrying or running errands, and I am experienced at caring for children having looked after him alone. What age are your daughters if you don't mind me asking?"

"Mae is three and Belle six, and they are the light of my life. The pair are currently off with my young brother Freddie, probably at the beach. Both are bright little buttons but have not had a lot of schooling as yet. Due to my incapacity…" She patted her hidden legs. "I am sorely in need of someone to take them in hand, as well as having someone to care for my needs at times."

"I cared for an older lady for quite some time, assisting her with bathing and dressing among other things, so have experience with that also." At the thought of Mrs. Pollock and the outcome of that experience Faith felt a small pang of regret. "My parents owned a guest house, so I gained my skills there."

"My, my, for someone so young you seem to have had a fair amount of experience at lots of things. Most young misses seem to spend a lot of time primping and gossiping among themselves."

That almost made Faith smile. Apart from the short time at her Papa's house there had been little time for such fanciful pastimes. "I promise you, I am a good worker, and am not the least bit interested in most amusements enjoyed by others of my age."

"Well, I will give you a chance to prove yourself, and the young fellow here can run small errands to earn his keep. Unfortunately, my husband did not leave me in a favourable position to give you a large stipend, but you can be sure you will be well fed and have a warm bed to sleep in while under my roof. Does that sound suitable to you?"

"Oh yes, that sounds perfect for us. Thank you so much. We will not disappoint you, I promise." Faith rose and just stopped herself from sinking into a curtsy. "Would you like us to start right away madam?"

"That will do perfectly well. My name is Mrs. Denton by the way. Now you go off and fetch whatever personal things you need to bring with you and come right back." She rang a small bell that sat on a table at her side and in a short time the housekeeper came in. "Mrs. Kipple will see you out. Will you need some assistance with carrying your belongings?"

"Oh no, thank you, madam. We do not have much to carry." As she said that, Faith remembered Matilda in the small yard and wondered just what they could do about her. With a small cough she asked hesitantly, "We do have a horse and a small cart, you would not have somewhere behind the house where she could be kept do you? She is well behaved," she added, as if that was important.

"Hmm, a horse, well, there is a stable behind the house and a small yard. Sadly, I had to part with my husband's horses after his demise, so Mrs. Kipple will show you before you leave and on thinking about it, that would work well, for you could take my daughters about in it. I take it you do know how to handle driving a vehicle."

"Oh yes, madam, I have had plenty of experience." What a lie. Faith had no idea how to put the harness on let alone drive the blessed cart. In her heart she had faith in Matilda and hoped she would not need a lot of assistance but would be willing to help her.

The small yard and stables were perfect, and Faith's heart felt lighter as they bid the housekeeper good day and promised to be back before nightfall. "Can you really drive the cart?" James asked with a laugh. "Perhaps it would be best if I did it."

"Of course, I can. How difficult can it be?" They hurried back to the lodging house and told the owner they were leaving for she had found employment. Leaving the address of Mrs. Denton's residence, she said, "Should Walter Finch, the man who arrived with us turn up, could you please direct him to this address as that is where we will be staying." How she hoped Walt would appear soon, with or without the brooch, which was of little importance to her now—all she wanted was Walt safe and sound.

The landlord eyed them oddly but put the piece of paper in a drawer behind his small counter. After packing their belongings, plus Walt's, they hauled everything down to where Matilda was nibbling on the meagre grass in the yard. With a whinny she bounded across to meet them. A man was loading logs onto the back of a dray and Faith went across to him and asked, "I beg your pardon sir, but we need assistance with harnessing our horse. Could you spare time to help us?"

Eyeing them up and down for a minute he then said, "It'll cost yer." Faith's heart dropped as she mentally counted what small funds they had left.

"I do not have much to give you sir, just what would you be asking?"

After lifting his tatty cap and scratching his head he said, "Got two pence?"

"Oh yes, kind sir, I can give you that and I thank you with all my heart." She had an idea that he was laughing at her but was past caring as he soon had Matilda in the harness and even helped toss their bags into the back. "Now we should go to let the constable know that we are leaving the lodging house. I would hate for Walt to return and not know where to find us."

"You really like him, don't you?" James asked with all the wisdom of a ten-year-old, as they settled themselves on the bench, with Bob sitting proudly between them. "I like Walt too, and hope that he comes back soon. He can probably work for Mrs. Denton as well."

It occurred to Faith that all their lives had taken an odd turn. Was it a mere matter of months when she was toiling away beneath her Ma's rule at Ballarat, not aware that she had a half brother or a different Pa? Whether Matilda sensed that Faith had no idea how to handle the cart and was on her best behaviour, the journey to their new home was uneventful.

Once they had settled her into what was a comfortable stable behind the house and ensured she had water and a generous share of what was left of her grain, they carried their bags inside. Mrs. Kipple took them all into the kitchen, including Bob where two girls were sitting at the large table, eating small pies. "This here is Mae," she gestured to the smallest who seemed disinterested in the newcomers as she carried on eating. Her curls the colour of straw fell in disarray around her shoulders.

When Belle the older girl was introduced, she asked loudly, "Who is this boy? I hope he is not going to be living here. I don't like small boys, they are rough."

"This is James, and I can assure you he has splendid manners and is gentle and kind. He knows more about most animals than I will ever know." Faith had an idea that this daughter would prove a handful.

"I don't care much for animals either, they are just as rough as boys. I don't like dogs." She eyed Bob as if he was covered in manure. "Keep him away from my cat, who does not like dogs either."

"Now, now, Belle, behave yourself. Faith here will be giving you lessons so that you become the brainiest girl in the world." Mrs. Kipple flapped a hand at the misbehaving child as a man entered, passed a quick eye over Faith and James and sat at the table. His straggly hair of dull brown flopped across his eyes which seemed not to bother him. Faith guessed him to be a bit older than Walt but the childish air about him made him seem younger. His waistcoat was undone showing a roll of fat hanging over the belt of his breeches.

"Where are your manners, young sir," Mrs. Kipple admonished the man. Turning to Faith she said, "Freddie here is the mistress's brother." She placed a plate with a large pie in front of him and he began to eat without saying a word of greeting.

Mrs. Kipple picked up one of their bags and then beckoned to Faith. As they followed her up the staircase, carrying everything they now owned, she said, "Pay Freddie no heed. He does not speak much and has no more sense than young Mae, but he will not bother you."

She showed them to a room on the same landing as their new employer. "Unfortunately, the boy will have to sleep in the same room, dear, I have made him up a small cot. The only other suitable accommodation is taken by Freddie, the

216

girls and their Mama, and myself. The gardener and other helpers do not live in." As she turned to leave, she said, "No doubt you are hungry. Come back down to the kitchen once you are settled and I will find you something to eat."

Later that night as she lay in the very comfortable bed, Faith pondered on the extraordinary turn of events. James went off to sleep the moment his head touched the pillow, but despite feeling weary, sleep evaded her. Walt as always was at the forefront of her thoughts. What had possessed him to go off after Harry, or more to the point why had he not returned at least by the next day and left the task of finding the Spaniard to the constables?

She blew out the candle, thumped the pillow and willed herself to sleep. A loud thump brought her to a sitting position. It seemed to have come from just outside her door. "Is someone there?" she called, slightly scared. Bob let out a small bark followed by a soft growl.

Her query was answered by a few soft grunts that could have been words. Climbing from bed she went over and put her ear to the door, calling again, "Who's there?" Still no answer, so she opened the door an inch so that she could peer out. Bob also peeped out. The landing was empty, but then Mrs. Kipple came out of the far room holding a candlestick.

Flapping a hand Faith's way, she whispered. "Have nay fear, 'tis simply Freddie. The stupid fellow tripped up the top stair—a regular happening."

Faith closed her door, patted Bob, told him to lie down and went back to her bed, now feeling uneasy. As much as Mrs. Kipple tried to reassure her, she felt quite unsettled. How could a full-grown man trip up the stairs, unless perhaps he had overindulged on spirits. The man she had thought was her father had often fallen over when he came in late at night after spending too long at the public house.

When at last sleep claimed her, her dreams were filled with Walt. Walt laughing at some silly happening while on the road, or how his face changed in the moment before he kissed her. Her body filled with such a longing as she had never experienced before. What if he never returned? How was she ever going to face life without him in it? She awoke with tears on her cheeks.

Chapter Twelve

Life was comparatively easy in the home of Mrs. Denton. A week went by and still no word from Walt, and Faith wondered if this would be her life from now on. Each morning she went to assist her employer with her bathing and dressing. The poor lady's legs were in a very bad state and could barely support her. "My dear husband encouraged me to ride, but sadly I fell rather badly just a few weeks before his passing and have been in this poor condition ever since," she explained while Faith assisted her.

After that chore she helped Mae with bathing and dressing. Belle had almost mastered the dressing part but needed a small amount of help. Faith then went to the parlour which was the only available room for schooling of sorts with the girls. Her employer kindly allowed James to join in the lessons. The first morning, as Faith had anticipated, Belle decided she was going to ignore Faith and with arms folded, stared out of the window. As luck would have it the bookcase lining one wall was filled with a fascinating variety of knowledge.

"What I will do is begin reading to judge what your interests are," Faith said, taking down a book on the history of the continent. Mae nestled at her side as she began to read. The child seemed to relish the closeness and at every opportunity liked to sit on Faith's knee as if the infant had been deprived of attention. Within about fifteen minutes of reading, Belle's interest seemed piqued, and she began asking questions. James of course was only interested in the wildlife, which was unlike that of any other continent, so he said.

A few days later Faith was teaching them how to read and the basics of arithmetic. As she was no great mathematician herself it was lucky that they were all so young with plenty of time to gain more knowledge as they grew older. Perhaps their Mama would see fit to employ a tutor as Belle grew of an age to learn more.

To Faith's surprise, one day Freddie entered the room while she was reading about the natives and how their lives had changed since the arrival of the white folk. Sighing loudly, he sat on a chair by the window, muttering unintelligibly, and then left as suddenly as he arrived. The following day he did the same, and Faith decided to ignore him, thinking that the poor fellow had little inside his head.

That seemed to be all that was expected of her. A man named Willie came in daily to do the nasty chores of emptying chamber pots and any other dirty jobs allocated. A cook also arrived daily to prepare the main meal of the day. Betty would never be another Bertha but was likeable in her way, although said little to anyone once she had found out what she was required to make. What Freddie did with his day she had no idea—but he did seem to spend a lot of time talking to the gardener who apparently came twice a week.

One blessing was that when the day came that Mrs. Denton suggested Faith take the girls for a drive, Willie assisted with harnessing Matilda. The mare was enjoying the benefits of being well fed, as Faith was overjoyed to learn that the local supplier of horse supplies had delivered grain and hay.

"Where would you like to go?" she asked as they went out through the gate. The sun was hidden behind clouds, but it promised to be a hot day, and perhaps stormy later.

"To the beach," Belle said loudly, and Mae agreed as she clapped her small hands. So, they headed to the shore. As it was Saturday a few families were either sitting idly around or strolling along the sands. One family played a crude game of cricket. How Faith envied them, as she wondered if such a life would ever come her way. It had seemed a possibility for a while when Walt began to show his apparent liking for her. Would she be forever looking after other people's children or old ladies?

Bob scampered about, frolicking in the shallows as they walked along the shoreline. Both girls had no desire to paddle, but James removed his shoes and socks and played with Bob. After a short walk Faith said, "Let us now go and see what Betty has prepared for our lunch." The girls decided to make a race of it with James and Bob at their heels and ran towards where they had left the cart. Both stopped and looked back to Faith. As she neared her heart did a somersault for there was no Matilda or cart in sight.

"Where is it?" James cried, as Faith looked about.

Walking across to a man who stood beside a small cart like theirs, Faith asked, "Excuse me sir, did you happen to see anyone driving our cart that I left here? I seem to recall you were here with your family when I tethered our mare."

"Why yes, I thought the man was your driver. He went in that direction." With a finger he gestured along the foreshore. "I do hope he did not take it against your orders, miss. To be honest he did not seem in full control of the reins."

Faith's insides did a complete somersault at that as she had an idea of just who it could be. "Was this man older than I, rather well built with dark hair?"

"Yes, that just about fits the description. I guess you know who it is then." As he said that a cart came careering towards them, the driver obviously having no control over it as it almost hit a small post. "That's him," she cried as Matilda stopped of her own accord a few yards away from where they all stood.

"Just what are you playing at, Freddie?" she screamed, sounding like a demented woman as she shook her fist. "How dare you take my cart and just look at my mare, she is covered in mud and breathing heavily. Get down this minute."

With a stupid grin on his face that she could easily have slapped he clumsily jumped down, leaving the reins dangling. James ran over and stood patting Matilda's nose as he muttered comforting words to her. Never in her life had Faith felt the desire to kill someone. With loathing in her heart, she stared at the idiot of a man who now stood beside the two girls who looked completely at odds with the whole situation.

"I thought it fun," was all Freddie said as he stood with hands deep in his pockets.

"Fun? Fun?" Faith's scream claimed the attention of a couple of nearby women. "Don't you dare do such a thing again.

What you did was a crime—do you understand?" All she could think was what could easily have happened if Matilda had taken it into her head to panic and run amok. Turning to the girls who seemed confused, she said sharply, "Come we will go home. Never mind about lunch, we will eat it when we get there."

The girls were silent as she assisted them into the cart. As Faith picked up the reins, Freddie turned to look seawards, and Faith could swear that he whistled off-tune. James patted Faith's knee and said low, "The fellow has not all his wits about him, Faith."

Not knowing what to say to that, she brushed a tear from her cheek as Bob licked her hand. All the way back what could easily have been the outcome played over in her head, and she wanted to weep. Why did something always have to occur to turn life upside down when things seemed to be going well?

When Faith stopped the cart outside the front door, Mrs. Kipple came out, wiping her hands on a cloth, calling, "My, my, back so soon."

"Freddie was very naughty," Belle decided to tell her, and Mae echoed her words, as Mrs. Kipple assisted the girls down.

"He did? My word, what did the fellow do now?"

224

Faith rubbed at her brow. "He decided to take my mare for a cavort," she said, not concealing her anger as she leant over and passed the picnic basket to the housekeeper. Without another word she flapped the reins and drove around to the stables.

James assisted her with the unharnessing as Willie was not about. "What shall we do?" James asked as he brushed Matilda's sides while she drank from the trough. "Do you want to move somewhere else?" The boy was too perceptive for his age. What she wanted right now was for Walt to walk through the gate and take her in his arms.

But she said, "We will have to ignore him, James. For where would we go?"

Sadly, her employer could see no wrong in her brother and his stupid ways. Mrs. Kipple had obviously relayed the unfortunate happenings of the day to her for when Faith attended to her needs later, she said, "You must forgive him, dear girl, for he is not as bright as you."

Not as bright? The man was downright stupid. Faith decided to ignore him from then on. As foreseen, a storm began to brew as they ate their evening meal and by the time Faith was lying in her bed it had become a full-blown tempest with thunder and lightning and a wind so fierce that she thought it would blow the windows clean out of their frames. James had no trouble sleeping, but Bob paced about the room for a while.

Sleep had just claimed Faith when Bob's growl woke her with a start. Her candle had burned low, but she could see his hackles raised as he stood with nose to the bottom of the door. The loudest of bangs was then followed by Freddie's bellowing unrecognisable words which made Bob begin to bark. Then her door flew open, and Freddie almost fell onto the carpet as he began to scream at Bob, whose bark grew louder.

"Shut the creature up," Freddie roared as he kicked out at Bob, who then made a grab for his trouser leg.

Ignoring the fact that she was in her nightgown Faith ran over and took Bob by his collar to pull him away as she tried to close the door in Freddie's face. This seemed to inflame Freddie for the foul stream of curses that came out of his mouth was such as she had never heard before. Reaching out he stopped her from closing the door.

Fearing that he would do Bob harm—or even attack her, Faith screamed, "Mrs. Kipple." The housekeeper seemed to be the only person who could handle this man who was not a man, merely a spoilt boy with little brain.

By now the ruckus had awakened James who came over and took Bob, pulling the unwilling dog to the other side of his bed out of harm's way.

Mrs. Kipple came running from her room, half into her dressing gown, crying, "What on earth is going on here?"

"Her stupid dog attacked me," Freddie shouted in the clearest voice Faith had ever heard come from his mouth. "Get it out of my house!"

"Now, now, calm down lad, and let me see you to your room." As she went to take his arm, he punched her in the face, almost knocking her off her feet. She seemed so stunned by this action that she reeled back, a fist to her mouth.

"Get them out of this house," he shouted as, fist raised, he approached Faith. "I don't want them here." Such was her anger by now that Faith glanced around for something to hit him with should he dare to attack her. Like some madman he stamped his foot, muttering obscenities again as dribble wetted his chin and shirtfront.

Faith slammed the door and beckoned to James. "Help me pull the dresser over in case he should dare to come in," she said in a low voice.

Without a word the boy assisted her as, with great difficulty, they pulled the furniture over. They just had it in place when Freddie began to thump on the door panels and scream about how he would kill her if she did not open the door. Sitting on the bed, with James at her side and Bob at their feet, they remained like this until it grew quieter outside, with just the occasional word from him. "Poor Mrs. Kipple," James whispered. "I hope she is all right."

"So do I, James, but we had to protect ourselves. I did not know what else to do, and she knows him better than we do."

After a while Freddie seemed to have gone away and Mrs. Kipple tapped on their door, calling, "Are ye all right in there, lass?"

"Yes, thank you," Faith lied.

"What will we do now?" James asked, as usual getting to the bottom of things.

Faith sighed. "I do not know, James. I fear we must leave. If he gets violent who knows what he will do to us, or Bob here." She patted the dog's head. Inwardly she also worried about Matilda, for in his present state of mind who knew what Freddie was capable of.

Before dawn Faith was up and dressed. Quickly she washed her hands and face in the small amount of cold water in her jug and went to shake James' shoulder. "Come James," she whispered. "I want to ensure that Matilda is all right and Bob must go out. We will go to the outhouse together."

Once they had both taken care of urgent needs, they went in to check on the mare. She appeared to have no aftereffects from yesterday's fiasco and munched happily on the grain James put in her feed bin.

As they were going back inside, Freddie came around the corner of the house. Stopping dead as he saw them, he shouted, "Still here? Get going. I don't want you here. And if that dog comes near me again, I will kill it."

Faith's insides did a somersault and fear made her tremble—not for herself but for the blameless dog, and James who was under her care, whether she wanted it or not. "It is not up to you," she said quietly, but then added, "Have no fear we are going, and you will have the house all to yourself again." Once the words were out of her mouth, she realised that without thought the decision had been made. How could they stay here while this madman had obviously taken a dislike to them for whatever reason?

"Are we really going?" James asked. "But where will we go?"

"I have been thinking. Perhaps we should go home now. What do you say? This journey now seems to have been foolish. If Walt were here, he might have other ideas, but I can see no other alternative for us. We are penniless and alone."

The housekeeper was waiting just inside the kitchen. A bruise had appeared on her cheek and Faith went to take her hand asking, "Are you alright?"

With a nod she said, "I will be fine dear, but I fear for you and the lad. The mistress is waiting in her room for your assistance. I suggest you tell her all that happened this past night, she may take heed of you. Her brother should be put into an institution. I feared this day would come when he would dare to attack a newcomer to the house."

"I simply cannot understand what I did for him to turn on me so." Faith shook her head.

"'Tis not your fault at all my dear girl. This is not the first time he has behaved in such a manner, but as I say, his sister can see no wrong in him."

The girls were seated at the table eating their breakfast. Mae was telling a story in her childish voice. They obviously had not been affected by the events of the night.

"So this has happened before?" Faith was sure it must have done for the whole fiasco and his hatred of them held no foundation. They had barely passed the time of day with him.

"I fear his behaviour is brought about by the storm, lass. Something in his mind seems to be unable to cope with such a change in the weather." Taking Faith's hand she asked, "Do ye think that you can cope with such behaviour?"

"No, we cannot. I have the boy to take care of, not to mention the animals who are really the property of a friend who has gone missing. I must go home but I fear we are penniless. That is the only reason I took on this employment, so we would have a place to stay in safety."

With a heavy sigh, she said, "Oh dear, I am so sorry. I have told the mistress many times that her brother should be where he can get proper care, but she will have none of it. Perhaps she will now see sense."

But unfortunately, she did not. When Faith asked, "Did you not hear the ruckus this past night caused by your brother?" Mrs. Denton waved a hand and tut-tutted a few times.

"The boy would not cause any bother, girl, he is meek and mild. His problem is simply that he does not see life as we all do."

"Meek and Mild? Nonsense. He attacked Mrs. Kipple. Did you not see the bruise on her cheek where he punched her?" Faith could not hold back her anger—how could this woman be so ignorant of her brother's faults, and to see him as a boy still was not normal.

"You talk nonsense. The foolish woman likely tripped. She has done so before."

"I witnessed the attack and if I had not barricaded the boy and myself in our room, he would have attacked us. There is no place in your home for us, and so I fear I must leave. I not only need to take care of my own safety but the boy's too. I will be leaving today."

"As you wish." The silly woman flapped a dismissive hand and Faith decided to go before finishing her usual expected tasks. Let the woman take care of herself, she huffed as she left.

Calling James, Faith went to their room and hastily packed their belongings, anger adding to her dilemma. James assisted her and together they dragged everything down the stairs. The cat made a rare appearance and hissed at Bob, who ignored it as usual.

Mrs. Kipple came from the kitchen and beckoned them inside. "You cannot leave without a decent meal. Sit yourselves down and eat some porridge, and I will prepare some food for you to take along with you."

Gratefully Faith ate, knowing it would be a while before they ate decent food again. "You are very kind, Mrs. Kipple, I am so sorry to be leaving like this but there is no way we can stay in such a household. His sister does not see faults that are clear to all."

"Now, have ye funds to see you to your destination?" she asked when the meal was finished.

Faith shook her head, for the first time ever feeling like a beggar, as she said, "We possess hardly any money at all. Most of the little I had was spent before we arrived here. We must make haste and get to our home in Melbourne as soon as we can."

"Tut, I cannot see ye go off with nothing, dear girl." Going to a drawer she took out a small purse and after poking about in it handed Faith a note and some cash, which she pushed into Faith's hands, saying, "I have no need of it. I will likely be here until I die, so you take it with my blessing and take care of yourselves."

Faith pushed what amounted to about four pounds into the pocket of her skirt as tears filled her eyes. "Thank you so much, you are the kindest person I have ever met." She reached to place a kiss on the woman's cheek.

"Go on with you and you be safe on your journey." As they turned to go, she called, "And take enough grain and some hay for the horse too. The mistress has little need of it."

When they reached the stable, Mae came at a run, calling, "Are we going for a ride again?"

"No, we will not see you again, Mae, you should go back inside now. Someone else will come and give you lessons I expect." Faith gave her a small push on the back.

Flopping onto the ground with a huff, she yelled, "I wanna come too."

"We cannot take you. Now be a good girl and go inside to Mrs. Kipple who will take care of you." Faith admitted to herself that apart from the housekeeper, young Mae was probably the only other person from this odd household that she would miss.

The child refused to budge so Faith went into the stable followed by James and Bob. As luck would have it, Willie was there and willing to assist with harnessing Matilda. "We have permission to take some fodder for the mare, Willie," she said, not caring if Mrs. Denton would agree.

"It's not much use to anyone here, Miss," he said with a grin as he piled as much hay into the cart as was possible and a sack of grain.

Faith sent James to fill the water bottles, and Willie helped toss their meagre possessions onto the cart on top of the hay. As they went out of the yard and through the gates, Mae was still sitting on the ground where they had left her, but now Belle was beside her trying to encourage her to rise.

"We must first go to the police station James, to let them know that we are changing our address again," Faith said, feeling weary and sad. He said nothing as they went along the streets that were now bustling with people going about their everyday business. She had a suspicion that he was not happy about returning home, perhaps wondering if he would get into trouble for leaving as he did without warning. "You stay here with Bob and look after Matilda," she said as she climbed down in front of the now familiar police office.

A young constable was behind the desk. He looked up with interest as she entered. "Good morrow to you Miss, how can I help you?" He grinned saucily.

"A short time ago I left a forwarding address here, on the chance that a young man by the name of Walter Finch might ask after my whereabouts. He left to chase after a person who had made off with some property of mine."

Scratching at his clean-shaven chin, he twisted his mouth as if in thought. "To be honest, Miss, I have only just begun my service here, but let me have a look through the book to see if I can find your information. What name do you go by if I may ask?"

After she gave her name, he began to flick through the pages of a ledger, a frown on his brow as he worked. "Walter chased after a man named Harry—the thief in question," she said in the hope that he might find what he was looking for. "He came here with us, and we were in lodgings for a while."

"Hmm, nope, can't seem to find anything here about a Walter Finch," he said with a shake of his head, and Faith's heart sank. "I just had a thought though." His chin took another scratching. "Just last evening a young fellow was brought in by a trooper who had been scouting the local area—the natives get up to mischief and we have to keep an eye on them." That was said with a laugh as if he had cracked a huge joke. Meanwhile Faith wished he would hurry. "There is little information about this joker, Miss, simply that he was escorted to the infirmary as he did not seem to know what he was up to. Perhaps you might visit there and see if this bloke is the fellow you are speaking of. Other than that, I suggest you come in tomorrow when someone might be able to assist you more."

"Thank you, I will do that." A small glimmer of hope began to spark inside Faith. It seemed too good to be true, but could this person be Walt? As she climbed onto the cart she said, "We will now go to the infirmary, James, for it seems a man was taken there who was found wandering, apparently lost. It is probably not Walter at all, but we must make sure in case it is him."

All the way to the infirmary her insides churned. It was more than likely a wild goose chase, but she felt the urge to check. What if Walt had been wandering around for all this time? It certainly would be an answer to why he hadn't returned.

"Can I come in with you?" James asked eagerly when Faith pulled Matilda to a halt in front of the infirmary where a few other vehicles were parked along the kerbside.

"All right. Give Matilda some hay to keep her busy. And you stay here, Bob." She patted the dog's head. Together they went inside and to the reception office. The nurse on duty was different to the others that were there before, and she looked up with interest when Faith said, "The young constable at the police station said that a man was sent here last evening after being found wandering about in the bushland, lost it seems. Would it be possible to meet him as I have been looking for a friend of mine who went off some time ago and feel it might be this man—or he might know something about my friend."

"Ah yes, he was in a bit of a state, didn't appear to know who he was or what he was doing out there alone. Good job the troopers came upon him, for who knows what end might have befallen him had he been left there. Appears he received a nasty knock on the head which doubtless caused a loss of memory." With a wave of the hand, she ordered, "Follow me."

Faith chewed on her thumb tip as they obeyed and traipsed after her along a corridor. She stopped beside a door and to Faith's surprise unlocked it, before saying. "I would not go inside if I was you, as you do not know if this one might be dangerous."

With fluttering heart, Faith peered around the door. The nurse held it just wide enough for her to see inside the room which was dimly lit as the blinds were drawn to keep out the sunlight. The figure on the bed did not look up as Faith called, "Walt, is that you?" As far as she could tell the man had an untidy beard. The top sheet covered his legs, and a bandage was wrapped around his head. "May I go closer to the bed?" she asked. "I cannot tell from here if it is my friend for if it is, then he has changed somewhat since I saw him last."

With a nod the nurse agreed, "But I will accompany you, and you stay here lad. You never know if he is likely to become violent." She tapped James on the shoulder. As they neared the bed, the nurse placed a hand on Faith's arm. "It seems he was given a bath which he did not take kindly to. His clothing was very raggedy, and his shoes worn down."

The man stirred and muttered a few words that Faith could not understand. As he opened his eyes, she knew instantly that it was Walt for she would know those eyes anywhere. Sadly, nothing else about him announced his identity. "Walt, it's Faith," she whispered. "What have you done to yourself? I have been very worried about you."

Raising his head an inch or so he stared at her without a flicker of recognition, and the nurse asked, "Are you certain this is the young man you are seeking?"

"Most certainly." Turning, she called, "James, come and see if you agree with me that this is Walter?"

This did not seem to please the nurse, but she said nothing as James approached the bed. He touched Walt's shoulder and urged, "Get up Walt, we need you. Bob is outside and Faith has learned to drive the cart and we have been looking after Matilda."

A small frown appeared on Walt's brow as he raised his head again, staring at first James and then Faith. "Matilda?" was all he said.

"Yes, don't you remember your mare, she is waiting outside for you and so is Bob." James gave Walt a small punch on the shoulder.

The nurse put a hand on James' arm as she said, "Come along outside with me and we will find the doctor on duty and get his opinion."

They followed her back to the office where she told them to take a seat and she would be back. "What do you think happened to Walt?" James asked.

"I have no idea, but I am so relieved that we have found him at last." Faith felt as if every part of her shook as she fretted over whether the doctor would let her take Walt from here. And if he did, what would she do if Walt had changed so much that he never recognised her again. Would he ever remember what had befallen him to bring him to such a condition?

It seemed an age before the nurse returned accompanied by a mid aged man wearing a white coat. Faith jumped up as he neared. "Can we take Walt please? I am certain that once he gets among familiar things his memory will be restored."

The doctor put a hand on her shoulder. "Now, now, miss. Let us not be hasty. The man you are obviously certain is your friend has been through a traumatic experience and might never recover from his loss of memory. Some people recover after a few days and others might take weeks. We have no idea how long he was wandering about in the bushland. When did you last see him?"

Faith had to work out how long it was since he left her and James to go after Harry. At times it seemed like months and at other times a mere matter of weeks. "It was only a few weeks ago," James told the doctor. "Faith took a job when Walt did not return, and we were in this horrible house for just a little while."

"What date is it?" Faith turned to ask the nurse who stood watching the exchange with a look of disinterest on her face.

"March has just arrived," she said.

"Please can we take my friend?" She knew she was now begging but her nerves were becoming jangled. "We are heading back to Melbourne to our home, and he will get all the care he needs there should he not recover soon," she assured the doctor. Saying this, she wondered if that would be so. At least Walt would have his brother and Alice.

"Do you have a change of clothing for this young person? His clothes were beyond repair I fear." Placing a hand on her arm, he urged, "But do not get your hopes up. First, I must examine him once again and check his wound. Now you run along and wait at the reception—oh and fetch any clothing you have."

Faith nodded a few times and gently pushed James before her. Together they went out to the cart. Bob woofed a few times and wagged his tail in pleasure as Faith rummaged about in Walt's bag, finding a shirt, a pair of trousers, but no shoes. It seemed Walt had not packed a second pair. "I hope his old ones are not too worn," she said to James as she bundled the clothes together. "You wait here with Bob, James." Leaving him she hurried back inside.

It seemed hours before the doctor came along the passage. Faith rose to meet him. With a wave of the hand he said, "In normal circumstances I would suggest you leave the young fellow here for a day or so, but as you seem determined to return to your home, I will release him into your care. Do not be too distressed if he does not recover his memory straight away, but I am hoping that being with you will help him."

A while later when Walt came towards her Faith could not resist throwing herself into his arms. "Oh Walt," she cried. "Let us go back to Melbourne." Sadly, he did not return her affectionate act but simply stood with his arms at his sides.

Chapter Thirteen

Walt went straight to Matilda and stroked her on the nose, as he mumbled words that Faith could not understand. But at least the fact that he seemed to recognise his mare gave her a small measure of hope. "Come, climb into the back, Walt, and I will drive," she said and without argument he obeyed, sitting beside Bob who was so excited he could not stop licking Walt's hand. This did not appear to bother him, nor did he seem concerned that Faith was driving.

The clothing she had found for him appeared to be loose on his tall frame and she guessed he had not eaten well as he wandered lost. "I fear we will need to find some lodging soon, James, as we have wasted a lot of time at the hospital." Faith blessed the housekeeper for her generous gift. Without it she knew they would have to sleep beneath the stars or if rain came, beneath the cart.

After steadily moving as the afternoon wore on, James suddenly said, "I think that is an inn ahead, Faith." The boy was right, and she breathed a sigh of relief. As luck would have it, they were able to rent a room. As it was an establishment for travellers, Faith was able to get Matilda settled behind the inn. They left her busily munching on her grain in a small yard.

The innkeeper eyed Walt with suspicion when he stood by as Faith secured the room. "Is he your husband?" he asked, and for a moment she wondered if she should say yes to that.

But as usual James forestalled her and told the man, "He's been lost in the bush, and we are taking him home. Someone bashed him on the head, and he can't remember a thing."

"Hush James." Faith gave him a look of reprimand. Mind you, she had to admit it likely appeared odd that Walt stood by and let her do all the talking. Usually, the womenfolk left it to their men. "We just need one room." Now she had found Walt again she was not about to let him out of her sight for a moment.

When they were served in the small dining room by a buxom girl similar in age and looks to Carrie, Walt ate the meal that was put in front of him. As Faith thought of that foolish girl, she had a momentary twinge of guilt. What if she now lay discarded somewhere, abandoned again by Harry?

Just a few men sat around talking idly. One of them sauntered across and began to question them on their journey. Faith knew he was just being cordial but wished he would leave them alone, for Walt stared up at him without answering.

"Don't say a lot, does he?" the man said, and Faith put a warning hand on James' knee, for she had already told him not to tell people why Walt was so quiet, figuring they might presume that he was not up to taking care of them. A woman travelling without a male for protection could attract unsavoury attention.

"My brother is not up to talking at the moment," she said. She had decided this would be the best excuse for them all sharing a room. The man grunted and went back to his table, obviously telling his companions Walt was not talkative, for they glanced across at him curiously.

As soon as they finished their meal, Faith hustled them out. Her next worry was ensuring Walt used the outhouse. That task completed they went up to their room, where James unwrapped the portion of meat for Bob that they had taken from each of their plates. He ate it with relish.

"Here, Walt, you sleep on this bed." Taking his arm, she encouraged him to sit on the side of one of the three narrow cots. "We had best take off your shoes," she encouraged as he went to lie down with them on. "You will be more comfortable." As she pulled his worn and tattered boots she

245

felt somewhat like a mother, and her heart sank as she wondered anew how long—or if ever—it would take for him to recover.

"Let me help." James gently put her aside and began to pull Walt's shirt over his head. "Lift your arms," he urged when Walt made no effort to assist him with the task. James turned to Faith and wrinkled his nose. "I think we had best let him keep his breeches on," he said as he pushed Walt back onto the blanket.

"Thank you, James, what would I do without you?" Faith pulled her frock over her head and lay down in her chemise. As she dragged her blanket over her, Bob jumped on her bed, planted a wet kiss on her face and then went across and lay beside Walt. That was how he stayed all night.

She must have dozed off when Walt's shout brought her to a sitting position. James was already sitting on the side of his cot. "I think he was having a bad dream," he said. "I wonder if he was remembering what happened to him out there on his own."

How Faith wished he would begin to talk and perhaps explain what had occurred in the time he was missing. Longing to go and lie beside him, she turned away and tried to go back to sleep. They would have a long drive the next day.

* * *

"My goodness, Faith, what have you been doing? You look exhausted. Where is Walt?" Alice looked past Faith and spotted Walt still sitting in the back of the cart. "Walter," she called, "Get yourself in here." When he appeared to ignore her, she turned to Faith again. "What in heaven's name is he doing sitting there as if he cannot hear me?" Taking Faith's arm, she pulled her into the hallway.

As quickly and as briefly as Faith could, she explained why Walt was in such a condition. "I thought it best if he was here with you and George, Alice, for he does not remember me at all. I considered that George would be more help to him than I seem to be."

Turning, Alice called out and her young kitchen girl came running. Alice immediately sent her to fetch George from the emporium. They went out to the cart and assisted Walt down. Alice seemed stunned that he said nothing as they guided him towards the house and along to the sitting room. Alice gave orders for someone to take care of Matilda and then ordered tea and sandwiches for them all. James sat quietly stroking Bob. Faith had a feeling that the boy was becoming nervous now that they neared home and perhaps his father's wrath.

Alice left them and Walt stared around the room. When she returned carrying baby Bridie a small flicker of awareness appeared on his face for one second. Faith felt sure she had done the right thing by coming here first. Not long later, when George came in at a near run, Walt stood and stretched out his arms.

A small flicker of what was likely jealousy stirred in Faith, for this was the first sign of Walt recognising anyone since they had found him in hospital. Why had he not done such for her? Rising, she said, "We will leave now for I must get home before dark. Our Pa does not know that we have returned. I feel sure Walt will recover now that he is with you."

As she and James left the room Walt made no move to follow her but sat beside his brother, who was talking to him in a low voice. Faith had decided it was probably best to leave Bob there in the hope that the dog would help Walt.

Alice gave orders for the mare to be brought around and as Faith climbed aboard, she said, "Come back in the morning and God willing you will see some improvement in Walt."

James had been unusually quiet, and Faith said, "You are not worried that our Pa will be angry with you, are you?"

"I think he might be." He said no more. As they drove through the gate, Faith pondered on all that had happened since they left this house. Darkness was falling, and all seemed unusually quiet.

As they climbed down, Chappie came around the corner. "My my, now here is a pleasant sight for sore eyes," he said as he stroked Matilda's nose. "They are just eating supper, so you go along inside, and I will take care of the mare. She looks all in."

"She certainly is, Chappie, it has been a long day and she has worked hard." Nerves made Faith tremble. "I expect our Papa has not been too well pleased with us, has he?"

"Well now, don't you fret girlie. There have been a few changes here since you went off." Turning to James he ruffled the boy's hair saying, "And you, young fellow have had the master in a proper stir. Get along in now and Edna will find you some supper. You are looking tired yourselves."

After giving Matilda a quick pat, Faith took James by the hand and went inside. She was only half sure it was to give him support and could well have been to boost her own confidence. Nerves plus tiredness made Faith weak. No one appeared to greet them so she continued to the dining room where she could hear voices.

To her utter astonishment her Ma sat beside their Papa, and it seemed to Faith they were in close conversation, and her Ma's face wore a smile such as she had never seen before. Polly sat opposite and it appeared that the three of them shared some amusing anecdote. Polly noticed Faith first and as her name burst from the lady's mouth the other two stared in amazement.

For a moment it seemed as if all three were struck dumb until her Ma exclaimed, "So, you have returned from your gadding about, have you? Did you find what you sought, Faith girl?"

Not knowing what to answer through her complete amazement at the apparent change in her Ma, Faith simply shook her head. Meanwhile their Pa jumped up and came around to grab James in a bear hug. "What do you think you were playing at you little scamp to run off like that without a word of explanation?" he said without malice as he shook him gently.

Polly then jumped up and came around to take Faith by the hand. "You look positively worn-out, Faith dear. Have you eaten?" As she asked that Edna bustled in with a tray bearing plates piled high with food. After nodding at the cook, she said, "Ah, come sit and eat, you can tell us all about your travels once you have rested."

Feeling as if she had wandered into a strange land, Faith did as asked and once she began to eat realised that she was ravenous. In between mouthfuls James gave them a garbled account of why they left, some of what had happened on their travels, what the dastardly Harry did to cause all the problems and finished by telling them that Walt could not remember anything.

"Oh, goodness me, where is the poor lad now?" Polly asked.

After explaining briefly that they had left Walt at his brother's home and finishing what was in fact a feast considering what they had eaten lately, Faith yawned. To her astonishment her Ma put a hand on her shoulder and said softly, "Come, let's get you to bed, girl, and you can continue your tale in the morning."

As if in a trance, Faith allowed herself to be led up the stairs and into her old bedroom which now seemed like a room fit for a princess. Her Ma helped her out of her bedraggled clothes and into a clean nightdress and then, once Faith was tucked in, sat beside her on the bed. "I daresay you are a bit puzzled by the changes here since you left, eh?" She patted the bedcover. "I decided it was foolish to deny myself a better life and came to realise that Bryce was a good and kind man who only saw to improve your lot in life as well as mine."

"I am so happy that you came to realise such, Mama. What do you plan to do next?"

Gert looked down at her hand resting on the bed, before saying, "He has asked me to wed him, and I think I will. After all, there seems little point now in me returning to our old life. I know I made that life hard for you, my daughter, and in his patient and fair way he explained to me that it was good for you to go off and find your own way in the world."

Hesitantly, fearing a rebuff, Faith put her arms about her Ma, as tears formed in her eyes.

Gert gently pushed Faith back onto her pillow, saying, "Now, now, no tears, girl. You get some sleep and we will talk more in the morning." Staring at the flickering light of the candle her Ma then said, "Your Papa is a competent man of business, but perhaps you did not know this, for he is a man of few words as you likely found. His current interest is in the purchase of land to resell to interested buyers. Along with another man of means in town they have big plans to build a grand hotel and I shall be there to advise him. He seems to think that I will be able to assist him in this venture." Leaving the candle burning on the bedside table she went out, closing the door behind her.

Although stunned by the differences in her Ma, and all the new things she had learnt about her Papa, Faith's last thought before sleep claimed her was of Walt. Would he still care for her if or when he recovered his memory? The sun was barely sending its light through the curtains when

James came in and jumped onto the side of her bed. Shaking her arm, he insisted that she wake up.

"Guess what?" Without waiting for her answer, he went on, "That bad 'un Harry is now in jail. Papa said the police came here soon after we left and when he told them Harry had run off, they sent troopers out to search for him. Not only did he steal your piece of jewelry, but he stole some of Papa's finest silver along with cash." He bounced up and down a few times and continued, "He's now in Melbourne jail and likely to be there for a while, Papa said."

"And is Papa upset with you for following me?" Faith sat up and put her feet to the floor.

"No, and I am sorry I did not tell him I was going. I think he was worried about both of us. Polly explained to him why you probably went away with Walt. I think Pa likes Walt. Do you think he might have recovered yet?" This was asked solemnly.

"Well, if you leave me now to attend to my bathing and dressing, the quicker we can get around to George and Alice's home to find out." Inside she was still all a flutter with anxiety.

As they all sat around the breakfast table, with James still chattering on about some of the things that had happened to them on their travels, the new maid came in looking flustered. "The constable who was

253

here before is back again, Master," she said. "He says he wishes to speak to you urgently." With a small jerky curtsy, she left the room.

"Now what?" Their Papa pushed his chair back and tossed his serviette onto the table, before leaving them looking at the doorway. After a few moments he returned wearing a strange expression on his face.

"What is troubling you now, Bryce?" Gert asked as she jumped up to go to his side where she put a hand on his arm. "What did he want that was so urgent?"

Sitting down with a jerk, he shook his head and then wiped at his forehead with his discarded napkin. "It seems that a young woman's body was found on the outskirts of Geelong. A group of native fellows reported finding her body while on their wanderings. The police have no suspicions that they had anything to do with the killing as they most certainly would not have reported it if that was the case. There were signs that she had been beaten severely around the head and shoulders. After the poor unfortunate soul's body was taken to the infirmary, a nurse recognised the lass from a previous visit. She apparently is the girl who ran off after Harry, so we can only presume it is young Carrie."

"But how did they know to come here, Bryce?" Gert asked, frowning.

254

With a huge sigh he rubbed at his forehead. "From the connection with Harry I presume. The poor girl must have been lying there for all this time." As if suddenly remembering, he turned to Faith to ask, "When was the last time you saw this girl?"

Frowning, Faith exchanged a glance with James, who saved her from an explanation by stating, "We took her to the infirmary because she got bitten by a spider, Papa. I'm sure it wouldn't have killed her. I looked it up in my book and the spiders here down south are not deadly. When we went back to see how she was, she had run after Harry again." James seemed totally bamboozled by this latest piece of news, while shock made Faith feel sick to her bones.

"Do you think that Harry had anything to do with her death, Papa?" Faith asked while deep down guessing it must have been that scoundrel. He likely did not want a girl chasing after him as she did. Then another thought hit—what if Walt's injury came about after a scuffle with Harry over Carrie?

With a shrug of his shoulders her Papa said, "I expect the constable will have more news once they have time to put the pieces together."

The moment she finished eating, Faith excused herself and went to get her bonnet. James followed her as she guessed he would. Before they went through the door,

James said, "The picture of my Mama has been taken down from the wall, Faith. I asked Papa where it was now, and he said that it was in the attic along with other unwanted furniture."

Faith was digesting that news when their Papa came from his study, saying, "Ah, you have not left yet. I almost forgot to give this to you my dear." He pulled something from the pocket of his jacket and proffered a small object towards Faith. "This was handed to me by the police. It seems that it was all that remained of the items that Harry stole. By a strange stroke of fortune, he still had it hidden somewhere about his body, so the robbers did not find it on his person when they attacked the stage."

As he placed the small sachet into her hand, Faith had no doubt that it was her long-lost brooch. Staring at her Papa in amazement, she said, "Why, thank you. I cannot believe that after all that has happened that this found its way back to where it belonged. Are you certain that you wish me to keep it? After all, it really was the property of James' mother, perhaps he should own it now, not me."

"Nonsense, child. It was given to you as a gift and remains such. Keep it safe and it will assist you and your young man in the future. As my only son, James will want for little in the future."

Impulsively she put her arms about his neck and for a moment he seemed flustered as she planted a kiss on his cheek, a cheek that turned ruddy. He then put her away from him and returned to his study as if in a great hurry.

"He is not used to a fuss," James said as he took her hand. Bemused by the turn of events she simply shook her head as she clutched the brooch now tucked into the small side pocket of her skirt.

They went around to the stable as Chappie came from within. "I guess you want the mare harnessed do you not?" he asked as he doffed his hat.

"Thank you, Chappie, that will be good of you. How does she fare? I was worried that she might suffer some ill effects from all the hard work we put her through."

With a grin he shook his head. "She's a fine little animal is that one. Her belly is full and she has rested well. I'll not be long, and you can get off." As he went to walk off, he turned back to ask, "Not thinking of going off on more travels, are you?"

"Goodness me, no. I think we have both had enough of traipsing around for now. I just need to ensure that Walt is well again, that is the priority."

Within ten minutes or so they were on their way to George's home. "What will we do if Walt does not ever get better?" James asked, setting Faith's mind off to fretting again. The same worry had haunted her sleep.

"We must think positive, James." Although she said the words, she was not so sure that she was capable of positive thoughts right now. Too much was happening, and her head was awhirl.

The young maid who answered George and Alice's door said, "The Mistress is upstairs tending the baby. She said I was to show you into the parlour when you arrived. She will be down shortly."

"Do you know where Walt is—the man who came with us from Geelong?" Disappointment filled Faith when she realised that he did not seem to be in the house.

"I think he went along to the store with the Master." Saying that she scurried off, leaving Faith to sit with her hands fiddling in agitation.

"That's probably a good thing, isn't it?" James asked as he sat beside her.

Faith simply shook her head, having no idea if it was or not. After about five minutes Alice came in. "Sorry I was not here to welcome you, Faith, but the baby needed my attention." She sat. "I expect you are worrying at where Walt is. George thought it a good idea to take him to the store, thinking perhaps it would bring back some memories."

"So, you are saying that he still cannot recall what happened to him in the time he was wandering?"

"George thinks that he remembers some things. He mentioned someone called Carrie. Do you know of her?"

Faith's hands flew to her cheeks. "Yes, she is the young girl who followed Harry and then ended up with us on the way to Geelong. Sadly, a constable came to our Papa's house and said that she had been found dead." A feeling of dread enveloped Faith and she could not understand just why. Surely Walt was not there when the girl was slain—could that be why her name was uppermost in his thoughts?

Alice looked baffled, obviously unable to grasp just why Walt should mention her. "My goodness, that is awful. Do the police have any idea of how the girl was killed?"

"It seems she had many wounds about her head and shoulders." Faith pressed her fingers to her eyes as a headache began to form behind them. "Do you think I can go to see Walt now?"

"I sent a boy to fetch George and him from the store. They should be here at any moment, Faith. Can I get you something, perhaps tea or cordial?"

Faith refused both, far too anxious for either. The baby began to cry, and Alice excused herself to go to check on her. "Walt will probably be lots better," James said, and Faith could do nothing but hope he was right.

After what seemed a very long time Faith heard voices coming from the hallway so rushed out to meet them. Bob ran to greet her with a wag of his tail, and Faith bent to stroke him. Walt looked far better that he had previously. The bandage had been removed from his head revealing a healing gash above his left eye. His clean shirt and breeches, plus good boots, were obviously owned by George. The beard had gone, making him look so much like the man she cared deeply for. "Walt, do you remember me or James here?" were the first words that sprang to her mind.

When he said in almost a whisper, "Faith, is that you?" she felt faint with relief and wrapped her arms about him. When his arms stayed at his sides, she stepped back to stare up at him.

"He seems to be recalling things little by little, Faith, so do not despair," George said. "I took him to see a physician friend of mine who assured me that his memory should return in full within at least another day or two."

Alice came down the stairs carrying Bridie, who waved to her father. "Let's all go into the parlour," she said, "and it might be a good idea to let Faith have some time alone with Walt." She gave George a look full of meaning.

"Why not go outside, it's not too hot," George suggested, and Faith blessed him for his kindness. "We will send our girl with refreshments."

Taking Walt's arm, she led him towards the door. James was about to follow them, but George put a restraining hand on his shoulder.

The sun shone through the branches of a huge tree at one side of the garden where there was a wooden bench. Walt sat beside Faith and for a moment stared up at the sky without speaking as he stroked Bob's head. When he said, "I believe I might have had a hand in killing that young Carrie," Faith's hands flew to her cheeks.

"No, no, Walt it was not you who did the dreadful deed but Harry. Do you recall that you followed him in the hope of retrieving a brooch that he stole from me? He also stole cash and valuable silver from our Papa. Why would you say you had something to do with Carrie's death?"

For a long time, he seemed to be struggling to remember events, then he said, "Yes, I was chasing him, wasn't I? Young Carrie went with him. But where were you, Faith? I do not remember why you were not with me."

Faith explained how he left her and James to trail after Harry in the hope of retrieving her stolen jewelry, and he seemed to be trying hard to make sense of

261

it, but her hopes rose higher when he said low, "I should not have left you Faith, I think I was foolish, but cannot recall just why I ended up faced with the Spaniard." Rubbing at the scar on his forehead he shook his head. "I do seem to remember that he attacked me." After another long pause when his brain seemed to be trying to remember events, he blurted, "Yes, he was attacking Carrie with a large branch, and she was screaming. I remember trying to take the weapon from him and we tussled—that's when I believe that he struck me." He touched his head wound again.

"So, you do see that Carrie's death was all due to his nastiness and nothing to do with you, don't you, Walt?"

"I try hard to recall details and sometimes everything is clear and then it seems to disappear." Alice's maid appeared with glasses of cordial and for a while they sat silently sipping their drinks.

"George said that his physician friend believes it will all come back to you very soon. Would you like to come and see Matilda?" Faith touched his hand.

"Where is she?" Standing, Walt placed his empty glass on the bench and looked around as if the mare was likely to appear. Rubbing at his eyes he said, "I can't understand why I left her." As if the thought suddenly occurred, he asked, "How did you bring her here?"

"Well, would you believe, I had to learn how to drive. She is a brave creature and put up with my sorry efforts, but she got us here in one piece and is having a well-deserved rest." Faith decided to leave the part of the tale about the idiot Freddie's escapade until a much later time. "Come, we will go and see her—I am certain that she will recognise you."

Walt's hand was slightly rough as he reached for her hand. "I have been a fool, Faith. I cannot begin to imagine what you have been through."

"Never mind that. You are here with me now and I promise I will always be here for you as long as you want me." Faith blushed as he pulled her hand to his mouth and pressed a kiss to her knuckle.

"I promise I will never be so foolish again. I cannot imagine what I was thinking of."

"I have something to show you." Faith pulled the small sachet from her pocket and held the brooch in the palm of her hand. "Do you recall that you went after Harry because he stole this from me?"

Taking it from her palm he turned it over in his hand and seemed to be searching for the truth. Then he said, "It was given to you by that Mrs. Pollock was it not?"

"Yes, it was, but in truth it was a gift from my Papa. It was all that was found on the Spaniard when he was arrested." Faith tucked it back into her pocket.

A slight frown still creased Walt's brow as, with Bob bounding at their side, they went around the back of the house to where Faith guessed George's stable boy had taken Matilda. The mare was hitched to a rail with her head in a bin enjoying a snack, but the moment that Walt said her name her head shot up and her ears pricked as she let out a loud whinny. As he went to her side and stroked her neck, she nuzzled his chest while he spoke softly to her.

James came running from the house. "I heard Matilda calling out," he said. "You see Walt, she will always recognise you."

Walt ruffled James' hair and his familiar grin that Faith loved so much appeared, bringing tears to her eyes. "Would you like to take us back to our Papa's home now Walt?" she asked. "You will be surprised at the change in my Ma who seems to have decided that Bryce Witherton is not such a bad person after all."

"Ah yes, your Ma," he said. "Will she stay here do you think? I remember that she came down with a thought to take you back home with her."

"We will see, but from what she told me, I feel she would like to stay with Bryce.

She even seemed to understand why I sought a better life here with him."

"And now you must decide whether you wish to stay here along with them both." That was put more as a question than a statement, before he pulled her around and into his arms.

"I will only ever want to go where you go, Walt," she whispered in the moment before his lips met hers. Vaguely she heard James let out a loud whoop before she lost herself in the magic that only Walt could create.

Chapter Fourteen

North of Melbourne 1866

"Mama, come quickly." Daniel came dashing into the kitchen on his sturdy four-year-old legs. Grasping Faith's skirt in his small hand he pulled hard.

Faith set Violet down on the floor and nodded to Bertha, who was in the process of preparing lunch, asking, "Keep an eye on her would you, please?" At one year old her daughter was still learning how to walk, but nevertheless managed to get into mischief regularly. Turning back to Daniel she wondered, "What is so urgent that I have to leave my chores to answer your call?"

"Papa says that Matilda is about to drop her new foal and you should come see." He swiped at his nose.

Faith took his hand and together they went out and across the yard to the barn. The foal was already there amid the straw, and Matilda being the excellent mother she was, bent her head to encourage the foal to rise. Daniel clapped his hands as he went onto his knees to stroke the mare's nose, telling her what a clever girl she was.

"What is it this time, Walt?" Faith asked, as she too stroked Matilda's sweaty neck.

Walt's grin was wide as he said, "Another filly. Our girl did us proud and was no bother at all." He pulled Faith up and put his arms about her, nuzzling her nose. "I think we can leave her alone now to look after her offspring. Come Daniel, let us go see how our other girl is faring? She should be due to foal at any time." He hoisted Daniel onto his shoulders and together they went out into the weak sunshine which warmed an otherwise chilly July day.

The mare Walt spoke of was nibbling at her hay in the smaller paddock nearer the house. Placing Daniel on the ground he leant on the fence and sighed. Faith put her arm about his waist and said with a smile, "You are content, aren't you, my love? I can hear it in your sigh of happiness that all is working out as planned and your dreams are fulfilled."

Walt turned and pulled her close. "I certainly am, and I hope that you have no regrets, darling Faith."

"Not one." They both turned at a small cough from behind them. "Ah, Mr. Sims, do you need assistance?" she asked. Although Sims had been wed to Bertha three years now, neither she nor Walt knew of any other name to call their new odd job man and stable hand. Despite for years thinking of him as a mere peddler who plied his wares around the diggings of Ballarat, it turned out he was an intelligent man of means. He and Bertha had willingly agreed to accompany Walt and Faith when they sold the lodging house that had been given to Faith by her Ma as a wedding gift.

"I was a' wondering if I should move the horses from the far paddock before the rains set in." he said, looking to the sky where the sun had now disappeared behind clouds.

"Good idea, Sims. Take young Percy with you." Walt turned and whistled, then asked, "Where is Bob?"

"He was in looking at his new batch of pups last time I saw him." Mr. Sims chuckled. "Never did see such a doting Papa as that one."

Walt whistled again, and Bob came at a run from the small shed behind the barn, followed by one of his sons from the bitch's litter from last year. "Take them with you, they might be of assistance."

When man and boy followed by the two dogs went off towards the back paddock, Walt looked towards the driveway, and said, "I think our visitors have arrived."

"Granma and Papa Bryce," Daniel squealed as he jumped up and down, "An' James." He took off as fast as his small legs could carry him to the gate at the house end of the driveway, and there he climbed onto the second rung to yell out his welcome.

"Oh, dear, they are early," Faith said. "I had best go and see if Bertha is managing with lunch."

Walt took her by the hand. "I will come with you. I need to wash this grime from my hands." Barely had they reached the kitchen door than Chappie was pulling the horses up by the gate. "I will leave you to greet them," he said as he went inside.

Bertha came out at the same time and handed Violet to Faith, saying, "I heard the carriage, and thought you might want your daughter with you to greet them. Everything is well under way for lunch so do not fret."

For the umpteenth time Faith wondered how she would have managed without Bertha. Chappie had Daniel up on the seat with him now as he drove the carriage into the yard and pulled up before the house. Climbing down, he placed Daniel on the ground before turning to open the door. James beat him to it and was already jumping down and pulling Daniel into his arms before coming to meet Faith.

"Look at you," she said. "I swear you have grown many inches since we saw you at Christmastide. Happy birthday, little brother. How does it feel to reach the ripe old age of fifteen?"

With a deep sigh, James placed Daniel on the ground. "Not so different to how I felt yesterday." He then took Violet from her arms and spun around, bringing squeals of pleasure, as he asked, "And how is my niece doing?"

Faith had no time to answer, for her Papa was assisting her Ma and three-year-old brother from the carriage. Nobody was more surprised than Faith when a son was born to her Ma. The boy was instantly recognisable as Faith's kin, which delighted her immensely. Much as she loved James, it was pleasing to have a sibling who shared her colouring and features and according to her Ma, shared her childhood traits.

As usual her Ma had no hug of welcome, and after a brief word to Chappie, handed young Jeremy to James with the order to care for him and hurried towards the house, saying over a shoulder, "I must speak to Bertha." Carrying Violet, James took Jeremy by the hand and followed her into the house, trailed by Daniel.

Faith's Papa simply shrugged his shoulders, and turning to Walt who had come out of the house, asked, "How is my fellow doing? Do you think he will be well primed for the Melbourne Trophy in October?"

"He is doing remarkably well, sir. I will ask Mac to bring him out later to show you how good he looks. The horse has just the right character for a long race such as the

Cup. He would go all day if we let him, for he is keen to run and will stay at it for hours if given the chance."

Bryce patted him on the back and turned to ask Faith, "And when is my next grandchild due, my daughter?"

Faith touched her stomach where signs of another baby were barely showing. "I think it will arrive in the new year, Papa. Probably late January."

Beaming, he walked to the yard and rested his elbows on the top fence rail. Walt joined him and for a moment they watched the mare as she dozed. "You did a mighty fine thing," he said after a long pause. "Well bred horses are a prized possession not only among the wealthy, for even the poorest of men have need for a good horse in this country. Any regrets about buying this place, my boy?"

Walt took Faith's hand when she too stood by the fence. "None whatsoever, sir, and I think Faith feels the same. It would all have been impossible without the gift of the lodging house, plus what my Uncle Dan bequeathed me."

"Ah, yes, that must have come as a great surprise did it not?"

"For certain. We all thought that his mine was not doing so well. After he died suddenly, you could have knocked me over with a feather to learn that he left it to me. A mine that I sold easily to another miner."

"And you had no idea that it was producing so much gold?"

"Never in a million years. My Ma and Pa thought he was simply digging because he knew no other way of life." Walt turned at a call from Bertha who stood at the kitchen door announcing that lunch was served. Walt put an arm about Faith's shoulders as they all walked to the house. "And I have to add that the brooch that caused such strife turned up trumps in the end by helping us to rebuild the house."

"What luck that you happened to find this place when on the way back to Ballarat. I swear I would have done just what you did, my boy, and snapped it up once you knew it was for sale. It was fate, was it not, to find a home with a creek nearby and a well already dug."

"It certainly was. And so near to the town. Melton has a post office, and already there is a school awaiting Daniel when he is of an age to go." They reached the kitchen door and her Papa turned to Faith and placed a hand on her shoulder. "You look a picture of health my daughter, so I hope that means that you are enjoying this pleasant life."

"It surely is a whole lot better than any of the time I spent in the old place." Faith nibbled on her lip before daring to ask, "And is my Ma as happy as she seems to be?"

For a moment her father looked over her head at the nearest tree that swayed in the wind that had suddenly blown up. "I think I can honestly say that she is, dear Faith. She was not the happiest when she found herself with child, but now she dotes on our youngest." With a nod of the head, he added, "Yes, she smiles more than she used to, and even told me in one special moment that she forgave my Mama for the way she treated her all those years ago. For your Mama to admit such a thing is surely a giant step is it not?"

Faith had no time to answer that as they were called into the dining room just as a few drops of rain began to fall. The youngsters were already seated, and James and Daniel were arguing about a creature that Daniel had found. It seemed to Faith sometimes that her son was more like James than her. "How are you liking college?" she asked when they were all seated around the table, and Bertha was serving with the help of their young maid.

James shrugged his shoulders as if in disinterest. "I have a good friend. He and I share an interest in wildlife and all the creatures, and one day we will write a book together." With a flippant flap of his hand, he went on, "Well he will do all the writing— I will provide the information."

"You will need to do better with your studies, lad, if you expect to become a great author." Their Pa shook a finger his way.

As always when they were all together there was a lot of arguing and chatter around the table. During a lull, Faith asked, "How is Polly faring, Papa?"

With a deep sigh, he shook his head. "Alas, she has deteriorated somewhat. She would dearly have liked to accompany us, but failing health keeps her to her bed. She sends her love of course." After a brief pause, he said, "By the bye, I heard some news from an acquaintance about that bad un' Harry. It seems he cannot keep himself out of trouble. Now he has been involved in a bid to escape from the confines of prison."

Faith and Walt exchanged a glance and Walt exclaimed, "I sincerely hope the bid failed, sir, for he is one cove we do not wish to see as a free man."

With a small laugh, Bryce said, "Have no fear, for it looks as if he will spend many years in jail where he belongs."

All too soon it was time for them to head off home. As they waved them on their way, more rain began to fall. Walt went off to help Mr. Sims and Percy settle the stabled horses for the night.

Later, after the children were in bed and asleep, Walt and Faith retired to their bedroom. As he closed the door behind them, he said, "It has been a busy day, my love. Come, I asked Sims and Percy to prepare a treat for you."

With raised brows, Faith said, "I wonder what it can be." Of course, she knew exactly what the treat was for earlier she had seen the men carrying water from the kitchen into the small dressing room adjoining their bedroom.

Not long later they both reclined in the tin tub that was just large enough to hold the two of them but ensured that there was little space between them and so meant that Faith was lying in Walt's arms while he caressed her. "Have I told you today how much I love you," he whispered at her ear, causing Faith to shiver.

"Yes, but you can tell me again my darling husband, as long as you keep reminding me every day for ever."

"That I will surely do my love, of that you can be certain."

The End

If you enjoyed this book, please leave the author a review.

Also published by BWL Publishing Inc.

Settlers Series:

Bk1. Mystic Mountains. Bk2. Distant Mountains.

Bk3.Challenging Mountains. Bk4. Annie's Choices.

Wild Heather Series:

Bk1. The Laird. Bk2. Travis.

Beneath Southern Skies Series:

Bk1. Lonely Pride. Bk2. A Dream for Lani. Bk3. Leah in Love (and Trouble).

Challenge the Heart Series:

Bk1.When Fate Decides. Bk2. A Heart in Conflict. Bk3. Kate's Dilemma.

Remnants of Dreams. Amid the Stars. When Destiny Calls.

Maddie and The Norseman. A Call Through Time. Powerful Destiny.

Laurel's Gift. Amethyst. Crying is for Babies. Sweet Bitterness.

Award winning author Tricia McGill spent her early days in London, England, and moved to Australia many years ago, settling near Melbourne. The youngest in a large, loving family she was never lonely or alone. Surrounded by avid readers, who encouraged her to read from an early age, is it any wonder she became a writer.

Tricia's love of animals has always shown up in her books. Tricia devotes as much time and money as she can spare to supporting worldwide conservation groups and is passionate about supporting those who do all they can to preserve our wildlife for future generations. She also volunteers for a local community group that helps disabled adults and children to connect to the internet with provided computer equipment.

BWL Publishing

bwlpublishing.ca